EVERLASTING LOVE

SHANICEXLOLA

Disclosure

Before you proceed, please note that some parts of this book are arousing, adventurous, and downright raunchy. I encourage you to read with an open mind to thoroughly enjoy the passion within.

xoxo, ShanicexLola

The odds were stacked against us, but I was destined for him.

The way he catered to every part of me heightened my outlook on love. I wouldn't dare deny that his allurement was a gift from a prevailing force up above... until the unexpected happened, threatening to tarnish our newfound connection.

Tell me every terrible thing you ever did and let me love you anyway.

Tears fell from my eyes as Grayson throat fucked me.

I looked up at him through glossy orbs and smiled internally as he caressed my cheeks with his thumb. He tried to refrain from moaning and letting his head fall back from the pleasure, but he failed when I cupped his balls.

Massaging his balls in my hand, I gagged on his dick, pushing him closer by his ass. He hated that, but he couldn't stop me if he wanted to, and he didn't want to. I could tell by the way he slowly stroked the inside of my mouth.

"Damn, woman," he cursed under his breath and entangled his fingers in my long, wavy hair.

"Stand," he pulled back and demanded, lifting me to my feet.

Smashing his lips into mine, he held me closely by the back of my neck. Our sexual tension fueled our aggression as we fought for control. Our tongues wrestled against each other's, then moved like they were in sync.

Loving him was easy and fucking him was always a thrill.

His dark brown skin up against my butterscotch complexion couldn't be taken for granted. He laid me on my bed and coached me to relax, but Grayson didn't understand. I couldn't just... *relax*.

Every time he pushed his massive dick inside of me, the pleasure and pressure combination shocked my body. I had to lift up occasionally to see what he was doing to me. With every deep stroke inside of me, I held back from crying over how good it felt.

He watched my juices coat his hard, thick dick as he rhythmically deep stroked inside of me. Though I wanted to run up the headboard to catch a break and my breath, I took it like a champ for him. Dick this good needed to be cherished, not avoided.

Wrapping my thighs around him, I pulled him

closer, gasping when my move caused him to go deeper. My mouth was wide open and dry until he kissed me. I played in his beard during a passionate kiss that made my lips tingle with excitement.

"Please," I whispered, panting between his soft, delicate pecks on my bottom lip and chin.

"What do you want?" He leaned down and spoke in my ear, his strokes never stopped or slowed down. They were powerful and steady; deep and sensual.

"You." I dug my nails into his back. "I love the way you fuck me."

We were naked and nearly on fire. The air was on and the ceiling fan above my bed rotated quickly, but it was no match for our body heat.

Raw sex was meant for exclusive relationships, and despite nothing being outright confirmed between us, we couldn't stop now.

I knew the first time he rubbed the head of his dick against my clit that he would drive me crazy. That was a little over two months ago, and since then, I'd broken all my rules for him.

"Release me, woman." He tried to break free of my legs locked around his lower back. "I need to taste this pussy."

Obliging, I spread my legs wide, only to be flipped onto my stomach with my wrists pinned to the top of the bed.

"Obsessed with your body," he murmured, placing wet kisses down my back. "Every inch of it, even the meaty thighs you be hating on," he said, and I laughed into the pillow.

Whenever I called my thighs fat, he corrected me and referred to them as *meaty* instead. He deemed them perfect, satisfying, and reminded me that they protected the good pussy between them—the pussy that he sometimes randomly whispered in my ear he couldn't get enough of.

Grayson kissed the top of my ass and my body tensed up, anxious for what was to come. Gently, he bit my ass cheek, and I giggled.

The things he did to me, no other man had ever taken their time to do to me.

Grayson touched me like I was the ultimate prize.

Fucked me like he would never get another opportunity to have me.

Made love to me like I was the only woman he'd ever been deeply inside of.

"Obsessed with you," he said. The air from his

whisper graced my ass before his tongue entered it. My body relaxed as I gasped. The sensation of his warm tongue brought tears to my eyes.

I tried to catch my breath, but I struggled to get it together. He demanded I arch my back while he had his way with me, then he rubbed my clit with his thumb.

"Grayson, I—" I gasped again, this time squeaking as my walls constricted around his dick. He'd entered me with ease; the feeling convinced me that he belonged inside of me.

From the first day we laid eyes on each other, our attraction to one another couldn't be ignored. Our dates were fun, our chemistry out of this world, and too much time together wasn't enough time to satisfy our hunger for each other. It wasn't the mind-blowing sex that made me fall in love with him, but it for damn sure heightened every intense feeling I felt for him.

My pussy developed a heartbeat every time I saw him; no one could convince me Grayson wasn't the one for me. And if he wasn't the man for me, he was the closest thing to it right now.

He pushed me flat on my stomach, his strokes consistent as his six-five, muscular frame towered over me. The heat of his torso braced my back, and I felt securer than ever.

"Shit," he groaned in my ear. I knew what that meant, and I loved hearing it. After multiple, back-to-back, body quivering orgasms threatened to numb my body, feeling his massive dick throb inside of me while he came was my favorite part.

Managing to escape his hold, I pushed him onto his back to massage and suck his balls just as he released.

I couldn't resist tracing the head of his dick over my soft, full lips. His happy ending seemed never-ending, and I was here for it all. Every drop of it.

"You're so fucking nasty." He caressed my cheek and flashed that handsome smile I loved.

I kissed the head of his dick and giggled. "More of you," I whispered just before deep throating his dick.

The red numbers on the digital clock across from my Queen-sized bed read: *4:25 a.m.*

Regardless of us being at it since 10 p.m., I wanted more of him.

I couldn't get enough.

"You awake?" I whispered from underneath the silk sheets.

My head rested on his chest while we cuddled. My arm was tucked around him as I listened to his heartbeat. Last time I looked at the clock, it was 6 a.m. In twenty-five minutes, the sun would rise. My blackout curtains were closed, but I shut my eyes tightly and envisioned one of the many times I stood in front of my window, curtains drawn while Grayson stood behind me. His gentle touch was as soothing and beautiful as admiring the sunrise.

"I'm here," he said, his voice groggily and low, yet still sensual, deep and enticing.

"I'm sorry I woke you up."

Grayson kissed his teeth. "No, you're not." He turned onto his side and tickled me. When we were together, I advised him to sleep while I was asleep. When I was awake and he was near, I wanted him. All of him, but especially his attention.

"I'm not but I am." I whined and climbed on top of him. The room may have been pitch black, but I could visualize his handsome features in any setting. Whether my eyes were open or closed, I saw him. "What were you dreaming about?" I pushed him onto his stomach and sat on his butt to massage his back.

He aired a deep sigh of relief as I applied pressure to his back with my elbows.

"My family. I've been dreaming about them a lot lately and I don't know why."

"Because you miss them," I suggested. Grayson's family lived in Miami, Florida. Because he part-owned two southern restaurant locations in Kentucky with his best friend, he didn't visit them often. He was just as close to his parents and little sister as I was to my parents and two sisters. I admired that they always talked on the phone or texted in a group chat throughout the day. Family meant a lot to me, and Grayson understood that firsthand.

"I do. I mean, I always miss them," he mumbled into the pillow, holding back from groaning over my thumbs pressing into his lower back. His tense body was loosening up. He worked too hard without enough play.

"I worry about Gianna a lot. She's in college now and I remember my college days like they were yesterday. I was unfocused and fucking up for a while before I got serious about my Management Master's. Our parents retired and moved to Miami for a fresh start, but I know they followed Gianna to make sure she doesn't bullshit around like I did." He chuckled to himself. "They're worried about her little ass, too."

"College is an experience. And that's what she has to do, experience."

"I feel you. I just miss her annoying ass. I want her to be good on her own. She's depended on us for so long."

"Do you think you give her enough credit to get through things and survive on her own?"

"Nah," he answered and laughed. "Guess I should work on giving her a little more, huh?"

"Just a little." I kissed his smooth, toned back and then fell over next to him. "But I love how you look out for her and check on her every other hour of the day," I teased him, giggling in his ear. "I love how you love and care for your family overall." I rubbed my fingers over his beard. "I might fuck around and lay off the birth control to make you a father one day." I couldn't believe that had just flew out of my mouth.

These days, I was so enraptured with loving him that I had to set an alarm to remember to take my little, blue pill every day.

Thankfully, my random outburst brought a boisterous laugh out of him—a laugh that made my heart smile.

"You're not ready for all that, and it's coo'. I'll be here when you are."

Silence fell between us after that. I didn't know how to respond. I wanted to confess that I loved him in this moment, but I was too much of a coward to go through with it. And that wasn't the only thing I needed to tell him.

His instincts about something going on with his little sister, Gianna, were right. I knew more than I'd put on, but my relationship with Grayson was fresh, and I didn't want to meddle or strain our connection.

While I was deep in thought, Grayson crashed his lips into mine. He slipped his tongue through my lips and I let him control our exchange. Even kissing him was a thrill, especially when he grabbed my neck and pulled me closer. This time, his hand massaged my breasts, then travelled down to my thighs. Slipping his hand between them, he pushed them apart and patted my wet pussy.

"Damn," he paused our kiss and murmured. "This pussy always juicy for me."

"Always," I assured.

Trapping his hand between my thighs, I rotated

my hips as he pressed two fingers against my clit. Our kiss resumed, and I rode the pad of his fingers until a final orgasm stripped the remaining energy I'd been holding onto.

"That's my girl," I heard him say as I drifted off to sleep.

"**M**an, whenever I stay over her crib, I make sure I wake up before her to cook her breakfast. If that ain't some bitch nigga—"

Don, my homeboy and business partner, broke out with hard laughter. Shit made me stop talking and kiss my teeth.

"This shit is real and you wanna play."

"You're in love, my brother. It's not rocket science. Everyone knew before you did."

"Chill out with all that." I kissed my teeth again. "Who is everyone?"

"Our crew at the Smokehouse," he said, referring to our employees. "A few of them asked me if you were okay. Said you haven't been tripping over production numbers like you usually do."

"I'm always in a good fucking mood lately, Don." I brushed my hand down my face with one hand, then flipped the pancake over with my free hand and sighed.

Chocolate chip pancakes were Molli's favorite and I'd learned how to make them from scratch for her. I couldn't even cook! But I was learning. For her.

"This is pure comedy, man," he said, and he was cracking up like he was watching a comedy special for real. I didn't appreciate that shit. If my phone wasn't on the other side of Molli's kitchen, I would've disconnected and snatched my AirPods from my ears.

"It's pathetic," I mumbled to myself as his laughter persisted.

"What's pathetic?" Her sweet voice aired behind me.

"Aye, I'll be there in a couple hours," I told Don. "Check your email and look over the reports I sent you."

"Yeah, yeah," he said and disconnected our call. I didn't trip over his neglect with sorting through our financial reports on time. I couldn't right now if

I wanted to.

I turned around to Molli standing in the middle of the kitchen rubbing her eyes. Her hair was wild and tousled over her head. One of my many T-shirts that she'd taken was hanging off her shoulders. The logo from the Smokehouse on the front of the shirt dangled past her knees.

To me, she was stunning in the mornings—the most beautiful I'd ever seen her. Molli's beauty was raw and uncut; I loved seeing her like that. It had taken her a while to stop kicking me out her crib after we had sex, and she wouldn't stay overnight at my condo for a long time. She had every excuse in the book until I shut that shit down and refused to keep being treated like a side nigga.

"Good morning, beautiful." I smiled at her, then turned back to the pancakes I was making for her. I never had to cook a lot for us. Around me, Molli hardly focused on her food long enough to finish a meal. She always fed me her food while talking my head off. "How are you feeling?"

She wrapped her arms around me, rubbing her soft hands over my six-pack. Lying her head on my back, she sighed deeply, tracing her lips against my skin.

"I'm good, baby. How are you?" Her small,

sweet voice always did it for me. It was enough to make me fall in love with her over and over again.

"Great." I cut the stove off and scooped her in my arms. Molli cracked up anytime I caught her off guard like that. Whenever I held her tightly in my arms and whisked her through the air, she squealed and giggled like she was having the time of her life.

For months I tried figuring out how she blew my mind with little shit like that. For months I failed to come up with any concrete answers besides the fact that I was in love with her.

"Put me down and feed me please. What have you been burning up in here?"

"Stop frontin' on me, woman." I put her down, then slapped her ass. "Like you weren't just complaining about those ten pounds you gained on account of my cooking," I said. "You know I'm getting good at this shit."

She swiped a strip of bacon, dodging my attempt to reel her into my arms again. "Mhm. You're right. Although I'm not sure if it's your cooking or those back shots you—"

"Ayo." I cut her off and chuckled into my fist. "Chill out and sit down while I fix your food." I aimed to kiss the side of her lips, but she turned her head, crashing her lips into mine.

Moaning as she slipped her tongue between my lips, she rubbed the side of my face and combed her fingers through my beard.

"Thank you. I needed that," she broke our kiss and whispered against my lips. I fucked around and gazed into her light brown eyes. That move stumped me every time.

Without trying to be, Molli was a dangerous woman. I didn't believe she understood the hold she had on me.

"Whatever you need, woman." I squeezed her thigh. Real talk, she could've gotten whatever she wanted out of me. "What's on your agenda for the day?" I asked, returning to fixing our plates.

"I have a book to finish." She pouted.

"*A World of Secrets*?"

"Hey, you remembered my title," she said, and I heard the wide smile on her face loud and clear.

I chuckled and turned around with our plates in my hands. Sliding her plate in front of her, I boasted with a grin as her eyes widened at the breakfast layout before her.

"I remember everything you tell me, Molli. I hear you. I listen to you."

I saw and heard her at all times, even when she wasn't around. I always found myself thinking back on our interactions, and I always caught something I may have missed. And trust me, I hardly missed out on anything about her.

Long story short, I kept up with her in all aspects. I didn't know why she continued to question that or act shocked that I was up on everything about her.

"I thought you finished that story the other day," I said.

We were at my crib when she bounced up and down on my lap, excited that she'd just completed an eighty-thousand-word novel. It was her fifth thriller novel and her best one yet. My words, not hers. I hadn't gotten around to reading the other ones yet, but *A World of Secrets* was deep, profound and an entertaining mystery from the very first page. Every time she finished a few chapters, she read them to me.

"I thought I finished it the other day, too."

As I sat across from her, she reached for my hand and closed her eyes. I spoke a quick prayer over our food, then slowly released her soft hand.

"Thank you for breakfast, baby," she cooed before diving back into the topic at hand. "I hesitated to turn it in, so I read it over a final time. I'm not sold on the epilogue."

"C'mon, Mol." I stabbed at my scrambled eggs and laughed at my little perfectionist. "Not only did you write three versions of the epilogue, you read the final version to me over six times."

"I'm sorry."

"Don't be. That unnecessary cliffhanger at the end drives me crazy every time I hear it, but I fuck with the story."

"Hey! It is not unnecessary." She cut her sparkling brown eyes at me. "Take that back."

"I take it back," I said, shrugging as I reached for my glass of OJ.

"You think it's unnecessary, for real? Should I change it?"

"Chill." I shook my head. "What's going on with you? Everything about your writing is necessary, Molli. I'm just fucking with you."

"You're right," she whispered and pushed her wild hair out of her face as she blushed. "Meet me halfway," she said, leaning across the table with her sweet lips puckered for a kiss.

"How much time do we have?" she broke our kiss to ask, crashing her lips into mine again—another one of her signature moves that I was in love with. "Before you have to leave for work," she finished.

"I have all the time you need," I said, rubbing my thumb along her cheek. "Why, what's up?"

"I have a surprise for you, and it'll be here in..." Molli hiked my shirt that she wore to her waist, exposing the shorts that stopped underneath her ass cheeks. Pulling her phone from her pocket, she checked the time and smiled. "About ten minutes."

"What's going down in ten minutes?"

"You'll have to wait and see." Right after she said that, she snatched a strip of bacon from her plate and ran out of kitchen.

"What the hell?" I mumbled to myself. "Damn, I love crazy women."

It wasn't even ten minutes later before the doorbell rang. Only a few minutes had passed before the loud, annoying melody from her doorbell echoed throughout her crib.

"Can you get that?!" she shouted from her master bedroom. We'd only been kicking it for a couple months and she had me answering her front door already, like I was a familiar face for whoever was outside of it. That didn't stop me from wiping my hands with a napkin and heading for the front door.

I looked out of the peephole and couldn't peep anything but her oval, bricked driveway and a few houses in the background, across the street. I should've expected that, though. It was positioned too high. I'd seen Molli struggle to stand on her toes to look out of it; she even jumped to check it once. Whoever was outside of the door was probably as short as her.

"Who is it?" I asked as I undid the bolts and turned the knob.

"Who do you want it to be, Bubble Butt?"

"No fucking way!" I yanked the door open to my aggravating, spoiled brat of a little sister grinning from ear to ear. I looked her up and down in awe. Her little ass had packed on a few pounds, but the weight looked good on her. Her short, dark brown curls shaped her puffy, high cheekbones.

She performed a quick two-step, then spun around and modeled a crop-top and jean shorts I didn't approve of. Her top showed too much stomach, along with a dangling diamond belly button ring that immediately pissed me off. Her shorts were too tight and the Ugg boots on her feet were unnecessary in this weather. "What the..." I stepped out onto the porch and looked around. She carried a pink backpack on her back, along with her phone and charger that she was never without.

"Boy, move." Gianna kissed her teeth and

nudged me aside. "Where is Molli? I have to officially meet her. She's such a sweetheart."

"What?!" I brushed my hand down my face and followed her inside. I closed the door behind me and snapped around to Molli skipping toward us. At the sight of each other, they squealed and jumped up and down in each other's arms. If I didn't know any better, I would've thought they were best friends and had been for years.

"Gia," I called out to her, trying to ask her what she was doing here. Not that I wasn't happy to see her; I'd been wanting to hang out with my little sister again since she went off to college in Miami.

The moment she graduated high school with honors and accepted a full-ride scholarship to Florida Memorial University, our parents rented a beach home out there to follow her. Gianna had no complaints there. She was the baby of our family and basked in that. Our parents being close-by meant she wouldn't want for anything. She wouldn't even experience the struggles of truly being a college student because they would run to her every rescue. I mentioned that to our parents, but they didn't want to hear it. Gianna was their baby girl, and they made sure she was happy and satisfied every minute of the day.

"Molli," I said after Gianna ignored me.

"He's jealous," Gianna whispered to her.

"Totally jealous." Molli snickered.

For Gianna to say I was jealous was a reach. I may have been confused on how we'd all gotten here and a little freaked out that my sister and the woman I loved knew each other, but I wasn't jealous. If anything, I was relieved they got along, and that Molli didn't think Gianna was a spoiled brat like everyone else did. But that also told me everything I needed to know about Molli. They were one in the same.

"Let me show you to the guest room," Molli said.

"Oh, no need for that. You need to help him pick his mouth up from the ground." Gia giggled, then rose up on her toes to kiss my cheek. "Just point me in the right direction and I'll settle right in."

Molli motioned down the hall and explained that a bathroom was in the guest room. The second floor to her home wasn't decorated yet, so she pretended like it didn't exist at the moment. After she pointed out the kitchen, the living room, and the back door that led to the screened in pool and backyard, she turned to me and smiled.

That adorable ass toothy smile fucked me up every time.

She waited until Gianna closed herself inside of the guest room and said, "She's here for spring break."

I stared into her bright, brown eyes and couldn't find the right words to respond.

"You told me you missed her the other night."

"So you reached out to her?" I asked, pulling her into my arms.

"I didn't actually. After we had that pillow fight a month back, and you posted a picture of me making a snow angel in all the cotton on your bedroom floor, without my permission might I add..." She paused to roll her eyes. I didn't trip, though, because a smile was attached to it. "She added me as a friend on Facebook and sent me a message."

"Last month?" I tickled her sides and shook my head. Her sexy giggle almost distracted me and my dick, but I remained strong. I didn't like being out of the know when it came to my family, but this was different. It was hard to explain what I was feeling, but everything about them connecting made me feel good. "I didn't even tag you in that photo."

"I take it she searched your friend's list and

found me." Molli laughed. "I used to do that to my sisters whenever I suspected they were dating someone new."

Silence fell between us as I stared at her. She cocked her head to the side as her eyes roamed the room, but she couldn't avoid me for long.

"What?" Her innocent voice emitted as a whisper. "Are you mad at me or something? I didn't mean to overstep my boundaries." All I could do was stare at her, even as she started from the beginning and dug deep into her explanation. "She sent me a message threatening to kill me if I hurt you. I must say the threat was written professionally. She even called me pretty at the end."

I covered my mouth with my fist and laughed. Gianna was just as overprotective of me as I was of her.

"I promised her I wouldn't and that was it. Then, I promised her I wouldn't tell you she threatened to run me over with her car if I ever fucked you over. But after you told me you missed her and were worried about her, I hit her up and invited her out here. She told me she wanted to surprise you for spring break and—"

"Molli." I towered over her and chuckled. She was talking too fast, approaching hyperventilation, and driving herself crazy trying to explain. "What boundaries?" I quipped. Lord knows I would let her do whatever she wanted to do, however she wanted to do it, and whenever she felt like it. And maybe one day, me giving her that much freedom with me would fuck me over. Who knew. All I knew was, right now, she could have her way and she could do no wrong.

"I'm not tripping." I rubbed my thumb over the center of her throat, then leaned down to kiss it. "Thank you. I'm glad she's here." That's all I could say. Inside, I was praising their new bond and hype fact that Gianna was here. I couldn't get her to leave that damn school and come visit me for anything. She acted like she was stuck there, and I knew she needed to get away. Her Facebook statues and quote reposting's told me more about her feelings than she did lately.

"Thank you," I repeated in Molli's ear and squeezed her ass. My phone rang from the kitchen and I sighed with my forehead against hers. "The Smokehouse has been packed all week. That's probably Don hitting me up asking where I am."

"Go on," she said, yet holding onto me tighter. "We'll be fine. I'll make sure she's comfortable, we'll have some girl time and maybe stop by the Smokehouse to eat later on, so you can hover around and watch us."

"I don't hover."

"Mhm. Sure you don't."

"You think I hover?"

"I think you're handsome," she said, escaping my arms and twirling around me. She sure knew how to distract me, and I loved letting her get away with it. "See you soon." She wrapped her arms around my neck, rubbing her face on my beard. It was cute shit like that—cute, little things like that, that made me fall deeper in love with her every second of the day.

She knew I had to shower and rush out without kissing her goodbye. A kiss goodbye never worked out for us anyway. During the time we'd been kicking it, I skipped out on work more than I ever had because I couldn't let her go. Whenever she was in my arms, it was hard releasing her.

And we never said we would see each other later, *soon* was a better term for our thirsty asses.

"See you soon." I kissed her forehead and forced myself to pull away.

Pulling away from her would never get easier for me.

Chapter 2

MOLLI

"**I**s he gone?" Gianna shouted from the guest room a few minutes after the front door closed.

"The coast is clear!" I returned, heading into the kitchen to clean up.

"Thank God. I'm starving." She rushed into the kitchen and picked off the plates we never got the chance to officially dig into. "My brother notices everything about me. I was scared he would..." Gianna stopped talking to stuff her mouth with a thick piece of pancake.

"Gianna, I don't want to get between you two or hide anything from—"

"I'm going to tell him, Molli. I promise I am,"

she said, looking up into my eyes. I couldn't tell if she was lying or not. Her glowing brown eyes mirrored her brother's and I got lost in them as my thoughts drifted to sweet recollections of him.

I closed my eyes tightly and smiled, then opened them to her staring me upside my head.

"You okay, girl?" she asked.

"Yeah." I sighed, shaking my thoughts of Grayson. "Look, he didn't trip when I told him we introduced ourselves to each other via Facebook Messenger last month." I laughed to myself. "He seemed relieved about it." I shrugged, still smiling like a fool in love. Gianna smiled, too. One thing I knew for a fact we had in common was how much we loved to see Grayson happy. "But Gianna I can't keep your secret from him. You have to tell him soon, because I have to tell him you confided in me about it and why if you don't. I have sisters and if they—" I stopped talking and shook my head. She knew where I was going with this.

"I know, I know." She dropped her fork and it banged against the plate. "Don't you think I know that? I know I put you in a weird position with my brother. I wasn't ready to tell my friends or anyone in my family for that matter, so I told you," she said and rolled her eyes, like I was scum or something. I was almost offended until she continued and said, "I can't afford a therapist on my own right now, my parents or Grayson would hire one for me, but I would have to tell them what's wrong. All I had was you. Talking to you was easy so I—" Before I knew it, she burst into tears, sobbing with her mouth wide open.

I tried to control my face, but I couldn't stop it from scrunching up at the food in her mouth. Her mascara clearly wasn't waterproof, and she pulled her lashes off before they streamed down her dark brown cheeks, right along with her tears and running mascara. Through all of that, Gianna was still a stunning girl. She was nineteen, beautiful as ever, and I knew she had to be smarter than she put on if she was going to school for a Bachelor's degree in Communications. Television Broadcasting to be exact.

She had to have had common sense. She shouldn't have been pregnant after her first year in college.

"I told him not to nut in me," she spoke through hard sobs. It took me a while to figure out what she said, but when I did, my eyes widened. I shook my head and shuddered at the thought.

"Okay, too much information." I covered my mouth, holding back a loud cackle.

"Oh, God." She swallowed her food while sniffling and trying to catch her breath. "I should've bought a Plan B."

"Gianna, snap out of it!" I circled around the island and shook her by her shoulders. "Let's talk about your next steps."

"I'm going to tell him!" she shouted at me, and I let it go. I knew she was undergoing a slew of emotions.

"Oh, I know you are," I said. I was going to make sure she kept her word on that. "Besides that, what are you going to do? Did you at least tell the father of your child that you're pregnant?"

"Yes, and he wants to keep it. He graduates from FMU in a few months and he's already planning a future for us. He tried to propose to me." She scoffed and held her hand up, flashing a small diamond ring, except it wasn't on her ring finger. It was on her middle finger instead.

"And you don't want that?" I side-eyed her, trying to figure her out, but that wasn't easy. Gianna was a difficult, fiery piece of work.

"I'm only nineteen, Molli." She wiped her wet

eyes with the back of her hand and resumed eating what was left on Grayson's plate. " And he's only twenty. He might think he's ready because he claims he wants a big family before he's thirty-years-old, but I don't think either of us are ready. I don't care what he says." Gianna rambled on about her and her boyfriend, Xavier, not being ready for a real commitment. To her, they were just having exclusive fun—exclusive fun that got complicated after a careless night of too much Hennessy.

Hennessy. The root of all evil, coming in right behind money.

According to Gianna, the condom broke during sex because it was defective. She argued me down about their being a recall on Magnum condoms. Gianna hardly took responsibility for her unexpected pregnancy.

"Do you love him?"

"Yes, and I know he loves me. But our love for each other isn't enough for a child. We need stability, a plan, and a lot of money for diapers. They're like twenty-five dollars a pop or something."

Finally, there was some common-sense kicking in. But although she was aware of all that, deciding on whether to keep the baby or not was a tough decision. It broke my heart that getting an abortion was an option for her.

"Did you tell him you're thinking about getting an abortion?" I asked, and she nodded.

"He's made it clear he doesn't want that," she said. "I wanted him to fight with me about it or break up with me to make my decision easier. But he only said he respects my decision and understand it's my body, and that we'll get through it all together."

"Damn," I whispered to myself, shaking my head. It felt as if her heavy heart and overbearing emotions were transferring to me.

My shoulders slouched as I tried to maintain my poker face. Gianna was crying her eyes out again, and I was standing in front of her frozen in place.

"I'm going to go take a shower. After that, I have to get some work done in my office. You're welcome to whatever you want in here. Make yourself at home, okay?" We stared at each other and nodded in unison.

Taking a step in the opposite direction, I doubled back to hug her. Gianna wept as I squeezed her in my arms, hoping I could piece the broken parts of her back together.

"Thank you for everything, Molli," she said. "I'll

clean up in here. It's the least I can do after all the trouble I've been putting you through."

"Right," I chimed, teasing her with a sly smile. "I'm here for you. Let me know if you need anything," I finished, then disappeared down the hall into my bedroom.

I needed to breathe freely without her around. To think clearly without looking at her and feeling bad while trying to ponder solutions for everything she was going through.

God. What have I gotten myself mixed up in?

"OH NO, SWEETHEART." MONA OPENED HER FRONT door and laughed in my face. The nerve of her to laugh at my pain. She wiggled her finger in my face and I wanted to snatch her stiletto shaped nail off. "Don't come over here looking like a sad puppy. I don't want to hear it."

Backing into her condo, she left the door wide open for me to enter. I locked the door behind me before following her into her living room and plopping down onto the white, fur love seat in the corner. The love seat was positioned by the window that overlooked the big, egg-shaped pond alongside her place. I was thankful her sheer curtains were drawn a bit; I liked staring out at the pond whenever I visited her.

"I need my sister right now." I blew a breath and pouted. "Please don't be my enemy. Not right now." I whined.

"Molli, spare me the dramatics today." She rolled her big brown eyes, still laughing at me. Scooting to the corner of the couch across from me, she tucked her feet under her butt, and I knew she was getting comfortable to tune in. "You sent that little girl a plane ticket."

"She's nineteen."

"Her age doesn't make her grown, and she for damn sure isn't acting like she's grown."

"Damn, girl." I smiled and side-eyed her as she snapped her neck with attitude. "Donovan done turned you into a lil' feisty thing, huh?"

"Mol, stop playing all the time. This is serious," she said, and I rolled my own damn eyes. I'd gone over her place to escape my current dilemma and hang out by my favorite window, possibly even come up with a solution for things before I left. But I hadn't gone over her place to be reminded of how I'd fucked up. I was caught in the mix of something complicated. And for once, it didn't have anything to do with me.

How ironic.

"Grayson is Donovan's best friend, or should I say brother? When this comes out—"

"You'll have to hear about it during pillow talk. Yeah, yeah. All I know is, you better defend my honor, okay!" I threw my arms in the air, letting them fall defeatedly onto my lap. "Gianna reached out to me and then we started talking from there. How was I supposed to know she would hit me with this?"

I didn't understand what it was about writers. Everyone wanted to tell us their business. Whether people were aware I was an author or not, I seemed to attract those who wanted to share their life's story with me. Still, I would've never thought something like this would happen to me.

"You didn't know, Mol. That's not what this is about. It's about you not telling him. You should've told him."

"Yeah," I mumbled to myself.

No use in arguing with the truth. I'd promised Gianna I would keep her secret. I was keen on being a woman of my word and didn't feel bad at the time I'd promised her. Now, a few weeks later, guilt was settling in. Gianna's pregnant ass was in town and I'd invited her. Grayson had been missing his little sister and little did he know, she needed him now, more than ever.

"I'll figure it out," I managed to say after getting out of my own head. Mona threw her hair in front of her and combed her fingers through it, styling it in a neat bun on top of her head.

"I know you will." She leaned back and smiled. "You always do."

My little sister always reminded me that I was in control. She was only younger than me by two and a half years, but it tripped me out how wise beyond her years she was. Mona should've been coming to me for advice and guidance, and she usually did, but I sought her out more than she reached out to me. I didn't know what I would do without my baby sister. Monika, our eldest sister, didn't know either. Mona kept our heads above water.

"Did you turn your book in?" She interrupted my genuine, goofy smile with that inquiry. My face straightened and my mood turned serious.

"I did." I sighed. "Finally."

"You drive me crazy, you know that? You're always on edge until your publisher's assistant emails you back and tells you the story is a go."

"It's nerve-racking waiting on their feedback."

"Your stories are always a go. Screw everyone else's feedback. How do you feel about your book?"

"I think it's my best book yet. I wrote my ass off and put my all into those characters. I love it."

"And that's all that matters," she said, snapping her fingers in circles. I nodded to agree and stared out of the window again. "When should I expect my advance copy?" she asked.

"I should have them in a few weeks," I beamed. Everything about holding the hard copy of my books in my hands brightened my world. It made all the hard work, joy, hassle, and stress to create it, worth it.

"I'm leaving," I said, looking from the window to my Apple Watch. I was overdue for Grayson's full lips on mine. I had one of his shirts on. The over-sized graphic tee draped over my jeans and smelled just like him, but it wasn't enough.

I needed to see him again.

I needed to loop my fingers through his as he squeezed my hand and refused to let go.

"I know you're going to the Smokehouse to see Grayson," she teased. "Only took one kiss in his office for you to lose your mind over him."

"Baby, trust me." I stood from the love seat and

twerked in place. "It was more than the kiss in his office that made me lose my mind."

It was true that I'd lusted over him after one glance in his direction on the first day I saw him. I went looking for my sister in the Smokehouse and wound up in Grayson's office with my lips against his. Our attraction to each other couldn't be ignored. Just as I was drawn to him, he was drawn to me.

All signs pointed to us being meant to be.

Mona chucked a pillow my way, but I ducked and dodged it. "Freak," she said, and I stuck my tongue out her before skipping to the door. "Call me later?" She shouted behind me.

"Duh!" I locked her front door behind me and headed for my car. Behind the steering wheel and tinted windows of my Lexus GX, I decided— decided that I wouldn't hold back my feelings for Grayson.

I decided I would take a different approach to loving him, one where I let him openly love and care for me without trying to run away like I always did.

I decided I wouldn't get distant with him and try to blame it on my writing career and tedious workload.

I decided I would love him with everything inside of me, and that meant not holding anything back from him, not even secrets I feared would put a strain on our new connection.

I decided to love him.

I just wanted to love him.

Desmond, our head chef at the Smokehouse, barged into my office and plopped down on a seat in front of my desk. Ever since Don promoted him, he'd been feeling himself. Before he got his new position, he knocked and waited to be told to enter. Today, I let him rock because I could tell something was on his mind.

"Mr. G, hear me out," he started.

"You can go ahead and drop the Mr., head chef." Leaning back in my chair, I chuckled and dropped my pen on my desk. "What's up?"

"Before you find out, I want you to hear it from me."

My eyebrows rose at that. I kept up with everything coming and going at our businesses—both locations. And not just with financial reports and promotion tools, everything. So, I was curious to know what Desmond thought he was letting me in on.

"Me and shorty who serve on weekends were kicking it," he said, brushing his hand down his face. "Stacey."

"All right." I side-eyed him.

I knew there was more to it. He had to know that me and Don were already up on that. Long as it didn't impact our employee's performance and they kept it professional at work, we minded our own. We didn't care what they did outside of work.

"She caught me kicking it with her cousin and all hell broke loose."

"When you say kicking it, you mean..." I paused, holding back from laughing. It was fucked up that he slipped up with Stacey's cousin, but the spooked look in his eyes told me everything I needed to know. Stacey was giving him hell for it.

"Yeah, I was drunk, and we were all at a party. Stacey caught us in the bath—" He shook his head and huffed. "Long story short, G, Stacey threatened to make me lose my job. She already keyed my car, recorded herself doing it, and put it on Facebook.

The only reason I didn't call twelve and press charges on her is because I know what I did was foul." I couldn't hold my chuckle in anymore, I had to release it. Desmond was an excellent chef, but he had some hood in him, and he couldn't mask that if he tried.

"Damn. I wonder what she's putting the cousin through."

"The cousin helped her key my car, man. They're good."

"I'm not too shocked about that," I mumbled to myself. "We got you, though. Your job is protected. I appreciate you for letting me know, though. I needed that laugh." Before I looked down at the paperwork on my desk again, I caught him frown at me.

"Aight. Thanks," he said, heading for the door.

"I'll talk to her when she comes in tomorrow. To let her know that kind of shit won't fly here."

"Good looking, G." He threw his hand up and walked out, closing my office door behind him.

I checked that the red light on my office phone was still on, then asked, "You heard that shit?" I was too lazy to go to Don's office to check in about an error on our reports; I'd called him five minutes before Desmond barged in my office.

"Impossible to miss it." Don scoffed. "I called it when you hired her. After fucking with Veronica, I can spot crazy from a mile away."

"He cheated with her cousin, man."

"You've done worse to women and I don't recall your car being keyed. You would've had a fit over a smudge on that Escalade."

"Aye, bro." I opened my top desk drawer for my brush and brushed over my beard. "This is not about me. I'm a changed man, and clearly, he ain't got it like me. My women respected me and my possessions."

"Man, get the fuck outta here," Don said and disconnected our call, but I heard his deep laughter from down the hall.

Just when I thought I was off the hook and could focus on sorting through paperwork, another interruption came through in the form of a call. My sister's name, and a picture of us on the day she graduated high school, popped up on my iPhone.

"What's up, Gia?" I answered, placing the phone between my ear and shoulder.

"I'm here to spend time with you," she said, her voice low and whiny. It was a shame how much of a spoiled brat she was. At this point in her life, she couldn't help it if she wanted to. "Do you know what else I could be doing for spring break?"

"I can imagine," I quipped and scoffed at the disturbing thoughts that came to mind. If I would've caught wind of half-naked pictures of her on the internet, I would've taken a trip to Miami Beach and dragged her ass home.

"Do you think we can have dinner tonight? Just you and me?" she asked, her voice softening and turning into a shaky whisper. My chest ached at the sound of that. I couldn't explain what it was, but I felt it all over me when the people closest to me were going through a hard time. In Gia's case, she was always happy go lucky about everything. If she was ever down about something, it didn't last for very long.

Something had been up with her for a few weeks now. She wasn't as chipper as she usually was, and I wished she would confide in about what was going on in her life so I could be there for her. I just wanted my happy go lucky little sister back.

"Yeah, wherever you wanna go, but I already know you're going to choose your favorite seafood spot."

"Rumors Restaurant, it is," she said.

"I should be out of here by seven, but if you need me before that—"

"I'm fine. I'm tired from my flight so I'm going to get some rest. I'll see you a little after seven."

"Bet. And you don't have to stay at Molli's crib, you know that, right? She won't be offended if you—"

"Oh my God." She laughed, and that made me smile. All I'd ever wanted for my family was joy. I was with and down for whatever made them happy. "Your place is boring, and you never have any good snacks there. I like Molli's place. Her guest room is huge, there's a pool in the backyard, and she has Swiss Rolls."

"So screw your loyalty to me over some Swiss Rolls and a few luxuries?"

"Hey, what can I say? I love it here. Have you seen her closet? We wear the same size in heels, and she doesn't care about me trying them on."

"Don't get comfortable. You're my sister, not hers."

"Ooo, do you think she'll introduce me to her sisters? I saw pictures of them on Facebook. They're really pretty."

"Gianna." I rubbed my temples and chuckled. She was falling for Molli just as fast as I had. I didn't blame Gia for liking her. Molli was easy to like, love and admire. Because she was a breath of fresh air, being around her felt easy and lighthearted. Molli talked to everyone she encountered like she'd known them her whole life.

"Have you met them?"

"I met one of them before I met Molli. She's with Donovan."

"Oh, the plot thickens. I can't wait to gossip to mommy about this."

"You will do no such thing, or I'll tell her what your GPA is."

"Asshole," she mumbled. "See you after seven," she said and hung up on me. And thank God she had, because the ultimate interruption followed suit in the form of the beautiful woman I was indisputably in love with.

Molli walked into my office like it was hers, locking the door behind her. Her hair was pinned in a bun on top of her head. A few long, wavy strands dangled past her smooth, light brown cheeks. Tucking them behind her ears, she blushed, then unbuttoned her long, beige trench coat. She sashayed toward me in six-inch heels, and I couldn't wait to rip her fishnet tights after I rubbed up her meaty thighs.

"Woman." I bit my fist and shook my head. She looked damn good, like always. And like always, my dick jumped at the sight of her.

"I want to hear you say it. Tell me you want me," she whispered, approaching me slowly. She was taking too long to make her way to me; my lips should've been on her neck already.

"I always want you." I tried to stand and snatch her thick ass in my arms, but she stopped me.

"Sit back," she said, twisting her hips around my desk. "Relax," she whispered in my ear when she finally reached me.

Molli straddled my lap and held my arms down. I always let her think she was in control for a while... until I took over, pinned her down, and had her begging for mercy.

"I miss you, and it's a damn shame how much. Feels like I haven't seen you in days." She rubbed my head, massaging my scalp with her fingers.

"I'm with you," I agreed.

Molli was never alone with her emotions, feelings, and deep need for me. I wanted her just as badly at all times, if not worse, every second of the day. If only she knew the depth of my cravings for her.

"Fuck me like you miss me." She kissed my cheek.

Grabbing her bun, I held her head back and kissed my favorite spot on her neck. My favorite spot was her preferred spot. It caused her to moan my name so loudly that I had to kiss her to muffle them.

"I have other plans for you right now." I ripped her tights and spread her legs further apart.

"Oh yeah? What are—" She gasped and held onto my arm as I rubbed her clit. We stared into each other's eyes, gradually leaning in until our lips met.

I parted her red, glossed lips with my tongue, anxious to savor her.

"Grayson," she paused our kiss and whispered. She held my hand to stop me from rubbing her clit, but that didn't stop her juices from running down my arm.

"I'm here," I assured her. She was looking at me like I wasn't real. Like our connection was all a dream. Although it felt like it most of the time, that shit was as real as it got.

"You might think I'm crazy for what I'm about to tell you. I know we're just getting started, but..."

"What is it?" I slid a finger inside of her, chuckling as her eyes rolled to the back of her head at the same time her head fell back. My finger eased right in, and she rotated her hips slowly as her walls constricted around it.

She was taking too long to tell me what I knew she needed to say.

Taking too long to tell me something I was anxious to wholeheartedly repeat back to her.

A knock on my office door made her lift her head. Molli gazed into my eyes and grinned. I loved how bad and bold she was. No one could tell me she wasn't the woman for me.

"Who's there?" I shouted with my eyes still trained on her.

"Mr. Steel? It's Amanda. Mr. Powell told me to talk to you about a few hours missing from my check."

"One moment, Amanda," Molli responded, and I only shook my head and laughed.

"Why are you so bad?"

"I came here to come." She kissed from my cheek, down to my lips. I knew exactly what she needed, and I wanted to give it to her. Standing with her attached to my lap, I cleared my desk to sit her on the edge of it.

"Remind me of our agreement when I'm at

work," I said, struggling to hold back from whipping my hard dick out and slapping it on her thigh. She fucked with how hard and heavy it got for her.

She reminded me of our agreement by pressing her lips together and pretending she tossed a key in the corner. I loved her loud moans whenever we took each other down in the privacy of our own homes, but I couldn't risk that here. We would've cleared the restaurant out if we showed out the way we wanted to.

I licked my lips before dropping to my knees and kissing her inner thighs. She rested her hand on my head, skimming her long nails through my low-cut.

"Tell me," I whispered against her wet, warm pussy. Unable to hold back anymore, I dug in headfirst, groaning over the sweet taste of her.

"Grayson," she whispered and sighed deeply. I took my time lapping at her clit and rolling my tongue around the inside of her pussy lips. I brought the purring sound I loved out of her, then eased a finger inside of her dripping wet pussy.

Positioning her legs over my shoulders, I squeezed her thighs. She couldn't control her legs from trembling, and I knew what was next.

"Grayson," she moaned my name repeatedly

while trying to push me back and clamp her legs together. When that didn't work, she put the collar of her trench coat in her mouth to stifle her moans as a powerful orgasm caused her body to convulse.

I sucked her clit until she couldn't take it anymore, until tears rolled down her cheeks and fell from her chin.

Standing, I wiped my mouth with the back of my hand and kissed her lips.

"You gotta go." I kissed from her chin, up to her cheek. "Before I risk it all and fuck the shit out of you right here and now," I whispered in her ear.

Standing from my desk, she situated her coat, securing the buttons while staring into my eyes.

"I'll tell you what I needed to tell you when you get home tonight," she said.

Home.

Home would always be wherever she was.

"Bet," I said and walked her to my office door to see her out. "When I get home," I confirmed.

I opened my office door to Amanda leaning on the wall across from it. She straightened her posture and cleared her throat, avoiding eye contact with us. Regardless of how quiet we tried to be, she'd heard something that had her twiddling her thumbs and acting uneasy.

"Later, handsome," Molli threw over her shoulder.

"Later... with yo fine ass." Shifting my tie around my neck, I stood aside for Amanda to head into my office. "All right. Let's take care of those hours you're missing."

Chapter 4

MOLLI

Strolling into Stardust's Poetry Lounge, I swayed around to the jazz tune the band played. Almost everyone in attendance had a drink in their hand, most of them frozen and colorful with an umbrella straw dipped in them.

Looking around for my best friend, Jana, I found her sitting at the bar, laughing with our favorite bartender. Making my way to her, I waved at a few people I knew across the lounge. For years, Stardust Lounge had been a second home for me. Everyone who frequented the lounge loved on each other and welcomed newcomers with open arms.

I was thankful I got inside without running into the bouncer who I had history with. Too much history if you'd asked me. What started out amazing between us, ended abruptly and confusing. I tried to avoid awkward run-ins with him at all costs.

"About time you got here." Jana jumped down from her stool when I approached her. She pulled me into her arms, and we swayed from side to side to the music, eventually jumping up and down like we hadn't seen each other in months. Truth was, we'd just caught a new movie together at the AMC theater on opening night, last week.

"You look beautiful. Is this new?" She fluffed my dress, fingering the soft, satin material.

"Yes. Pretty Little Thing has been getting all my money lately."

"I feel you, girl. Same here." She threw her head back and cackled as we took our seats at the bar. "I got this halter top from there."

"You're drunk," I said. No way she was laughing that hard over our excessive shopping at Pretty Little Thing.

"I am not!" She waved me off, her brown eyes getting glossier by the minute. "James, two more Pink Panties, please." James flashed his pearly white smile and held his thumb up. I knew how strong James made his drinks. He took care of his people's guilty pleasure when we visited the bar, and we took care of him with generous tips.

"How many have you had already, J?" She downed the last bit of her last drink, swallowed hard, then revealed, "Three."

"Okay, spill it. What's going on with you tonight?" I should've known it was something before I arrived and saw her like this.

A few hours prior, she'd sent me a simple text with a time to meet up at our spot. The end of the text said she needed me. But hey, we'd always been dramatic like that. Since the moment we crossed paths three years ago at Stardust Lounge, we knew we were soulmates in friend form. Aside from my sisters, I trusted her with my life. Our bond was a godsend.

"I agreed to meet Quinton's grandma tomorrow. Correction, I agreed to dinner at her house with his sister there, too," she said, and my eyes widened. "Exactly. I've bumped into his sister before. We sort of met in passing, so I'm not freaking out over officially meeting her. She seems sweet. But his grandma, Mol? The woman who raised him. The woman who means everything to him. I'm not ready to meet her."

"Why'd you agree to it if you weren't ready?"

"In my defense, it was a set-up. He'd just gotten done putting it down and I was relishing in the bliss of that when I agreed... a week ago. Time flew, Mol. Flew! I thought I could get myself ready for this, but I'm not ready. I know how much she means to him and—"

"First of all," I cut her off and shook my head. I tried to keep up with how fast she spoke without laughing at her pain. Jana was bad ass. She was tough, confident and firm with everything she wanted to do. Seeing her panic like this was odd and comical.

"Do you know how much you mean to him?" I asked. "No, you can't compare to his love for his grandmother, but he cares about you too, J. He cares about you and loves you. And from what you've told me, he's been wanting you to meet her for a while now. She'll love you because he does. But most of all, she'll love you because of who you are. What's not to love? You're amazing."

"Wow," she whispered, holding back the tears that brimmed in her eyes as she looked over at me. "Thank you for that. But I was wondering if you could call me tomorrow and fake an emergency."

"Absolutely not." I waved her off. "Thank you, James." I smiled as he slid our drinks in front of us.

"All that good material I just gave you and you ruined it. You were supposed to thrive off that."

"Friend—" She whined.

"Nope. No excuses. You love him, right? You have to continually prove it. It's an everyday commitment. You will meet his grandmother and she will love you. Period."

"Fine." She pouted and took a swig of her fresh drink. "But your tone is a little judgey when it shouldn't be, especially if you still haven't told Grayson you love him."

"This is not about me."

"What's stopping you?"

"I almost did earlier today. I chickened out. I'm going to try again tonight." I said it with so much confidence that I actually believed it. Fear set in quickly. My breathing hitched, and I almost screamed from the pressure I'd been placing myself under to tell him. "You don't think it's too soon?"

Jana scoffed. "As if we can control when we fall in love with someone. I learned that the hard way myself." I couldn't argue with that, so I didn't. I also didn't tell her about Grayson's sister being pregnant, in town, and staying in my guest room. Only my sisters knew the depths of that.

"I'm going to tell him. I only hope he feels the

same way I do, you know? I feel love in his touch, with the way he cares for me, and how he looks at me." I exhaled deeply. "We're just getting started, J," I said. "We're moving faster than we can control." I looked down at my lap and smiled. "But, still, we're just getting started."

Jana grabbed my shoulders, forcing me to look up into her intense, glossy eyes. "You're stuck right now. In order to move forward with your emotions, you have to tell him."

"Look at you." I grinned. "All drunk and poetic n'shit."

"Story of my life for the last week," she muttered.

"What's up, beautiful?" A deep voice that used to make my knees weak spoke in my ear and made me cringe.

At the same time, my heart fluttered. I knew I would always care about *him* no matter how much I despised the memories of what he'd put me through.

"Keenan," I responded dryly. That was the only greeting I could muster for him.

"How are you?" He asked. I looked up at him smiling broadly like a maniac. Keenan was still fine as ever.

Some things never changed.

His bouncer attire was all black, and his shirt was a size too small, hugging and showcasing his muscular torso. Every time I visited the bar while he was working, he tried to hit on me like there was another chance in hell he would ever have me. In any way. Ever again.

Kennan's milk chocolate skin used to reel me in every time I saw him. Every time he'd towered over me, I couldn't help but lift my hand to his handsome face to caress his cheek.

That part had definitely changed.

After discovering he'd cheated on me over five times while we were supposed to be devoted to each other, I fought the urge to slap him every time I saw him.

"She's good," Jana blurted and scowled at him. "And she's through with your sorry ass." My two-year relationship with Kennan happened before I met Jana, but past stories I'd told her about him pissed her off like it happened yesterday.

Jumping down from her stool, she pulled my arm to the fluorescent dance floor. The trumpet player of the band had been showing out during their jazz compilation. It was fine time to dance the night away while ignoring Kennan and pondering ways to tell Grayson I was madly in love with him.

I RETURNED HOME TO A QUIET HOME.

Too quiet.

Grayson's Escalade was parked curbside out front, but he was missing. I was used to him either sitting at the center island in the kitchen, watching ESPN on the small flat screen television above the stove while working from his laptop, or in my bedroom with his dick standing up, waiting on me to sit on it. Since I was tipsy and longing for him, I would've preferred the latter tonight, but Grayson was missing.

I knocked on the guest room door and whispered Gianna's name. Sniffles responded before she said, "Come in."

Cracking the door open, I slid inside and closed the door behind me.

"Are you okay?" I inched toward the end of the bed and laid on the suede, padded bed bench. The shutters were partially open; light from one of the night lamps in my yard illuminated the room a bit. Gianna was buried underneath the comforter. Now that I was inside of the room, I heard her heavy sobs loud and clear.

"I told him."

"How'd it go?" I asked. Truth was, I didn't know what else to say. Of course, I was curious to know how he took the news, but what else was there to say. I had nothing.

Coming from underneath the comforter, she sat up on the bed and sighed.

"My brother has always been my biggest supporter. He never puts me down about anything and this was no different, but he's really disappointed in me, Molli." She broke down crying in her hands, and my heart ached for her.

"Is that what he said to you?"

"He didn't say those exact words, but he didn't have to. I saw it in his eyes. He asked me what was next for me and when I told him, he looked at me like he hated me."

"What's next?" I stood and walked around the bed. On the nightstand next to the bed, I dug into one of the drawers and pulled out a box of tissue. "Does he mean your next steps in the pregnancy? What did you say?"

"He knows I don't want children. Not any time soon, anyway. I told him I'm getting an abortion."

"Oh no, Gianna." Tears welled in my eyes before I could control them.

She'd decided.

The thought of her aborting her baby made me feel physically sick. It made me think of my miscarriage that I never told anyone about. I convinced myself it was for the greater good, especially since Kennan couldn't get it together. Despite me trying to convince myself that it was for the best, it still hurt and took me a while to get over.

Kennan and I didn't need to have a child together. Our relationship was toxic, and he didn't know how to keep his mediocre dick in his pants. But deep down, losing my baby broke my heart. I still thought about it every night. Sometimes I heard babies cry in my sleep. I imagined an abortion would haunt her more than a miscarriage out of my control did.

"Are you sure that's something you want to do?"

Gianna buried her wet face in a pillow on her lap. "No." She cried. "I thought I was sure but I'm not anymore."

"Right now, in this moment, what are you sure about?" I cuddled closer to her. She needed someone to hold onto her tightly, even if it was her big brother's unofficial girlfriend.

"I'm sure about finishing school," she said. I thought more would come after that, but that was all she had right now, and I understood.

"With whatever you decide to do about the baby, you will figure the rest out. You'll finish school no matter what, because that's what you want to do. You'll figure it all out."

She snickered, then scoffed at herself. "You think so? That's a lot of belief in someone you hardly know."

"Your brother has told me a lot of stories about how smart and brilliant you are. I know enough."

Resting her head on my shoulder, she whispered, "Thank you." Gianna sniffled a few more times until they turned into light snores. I rubbed through her short curls and smiled while thinking about my sisters. If it wasn't for their guidance throughout my thirty-one years of life, especially my older sister Monika, I would've struggled harder through a lot of unfortunate circumstances and hardships. I wondered if Gianna knew how lucky she was to have a brother like Grayson who thought the world of her.

When Gianna's snores picked up, I snuck from underneath her and tucked her in. I dipped out of the guest room anxious to find Grayson. My tipsiness had faded, and now, I wanted to get drunk on him.

My instincts led me out of the back door to my screened in patio, pool and jacuzzi. The purple lights I had installed inside of the pool, along with the lavender plants surrounding the corners of the patio provided instant peace.

Grayson sat by the pool with his feet in. Steam floated above it, indicating he'd turned on the heat.

"Grayson," I whispered.

"Just come to me," he said, and a huff followed suit.

I paced to him, kicked my Fenty slides off, and sat as closely to him as I could get. I moaned lightly as I put my feet in the water. The wind was blowing just right, and the warm water was an amazing addition. No wonder he was out here. The vibe of the night, mixed with the water and lights, felt magical. The gleaming stars in the background perfected it all.

"Did you turn your book in?"

"I did." Thinking about it made a smile curl my lips. I took pride in my beautiful two-story home because half of the royalties I'd earn thus far had paid for it. Ultimately, I was proud of how far my gift had taken me.

"Good." He reached for my hand, squeezing it in his when he grabbed onto it. His gaze was focused on the water. The small ripples in it were visually addictive.

"Grayson, I'm sorry I—"

"Why are you always apologizing? Your intentions were pure, right?"

"Yes, they are," I said. "They always are."

"Okay then."

"Okay then," I repeated.

"Look at me," he requested, and when I did, his glistening, dark eyes made me want to melt against him. "I love you, Molli. And I know you love me, too."

"I do."

"Tell me."

"I love you, Grayson," I admitted. "And I thought it was too soon to be in love with you like this. After being cheated on, manipulated and betrayed in the past, I thought I would never give in to love again. But here I am, giving in and loving you. Wanting to be a part of everything that has to do with you."

His straight face transformed into a smile—a handsome, infectious smile that had the seat of my panties soaked.

After kissing the top of my hand, he pressed his lips to my forehead and sighed.

"I knew she was pregnant. The lil' nigga she's with called me last week. Said he copped my number from her phone."

"What?!" My mouth fell open as I blinked rapidly. "You knew?"

"I didn't want to believe it. I guess I was in denial until she told me herself."

"What did you say to him? From what little she told me about him, he seems to really care about her."

"He does." Grayson nodded. "I still want to kill him, though. And that's what I told him."

Without another word, I rose on my knees to wrap my arms around his neck. I kissed his cheek and snuggled my face against his neck while playing in his beard.

"She has to figure things out on her own, but we'll be here for her."

"We'll?"

"Yes. I'm not going anywhere."

"Okay then." He turned his head to kiss my forehead again.

"Okay then," I whispered and laid my head on his shoulder.

Chapter 5
GRAYSON

I knew bacon when I smelled bacon. And the smell of bacon had awakened me, attempting to summon me out of my sleep and drag me to the kitchen.

I stretched my arms out and felt Molli beside me. Though I felt her, I couldn't see her because she slept buried underneath blankets and a dozen pillows. She liked having the room freezing cold while she slept too, forcing me to get used to the rotating ceiling fan above us.

"Come in," she mumbled from underneath the comforter. I chuckled every morning she invited me into her big pile of warmth.

"Good morning, beautiful." I massaged her ass

while staring at her. Her eyes were closed, and a smile stretched across her face.

"Good morning, you," she whispered, slowly peeling her eyes open. In the mornings when she first woke up, they were brighter and browner than I'd ever seen them. "How are you?" She ran the back of her soft hand down my cheek.

"I'm coo'." I grabbed onto her hand and kissed the top of it. "You?"

"I miss you."

"I'm right here."

"When has that ever helped my case?"

All I returned was a wide ass grin. She knew how to pull it out of me.

"What time is work today?" she asked. Her eyes were pinned on me as she rubbed through my beard. Unlike other women I'd kicked it with, Molli never complained about my workload. She was just as busy as me, if not busier. That shit was sexy, even sexier how we effortlessly made time for each other.

"I'm taking the day off. Going to spend it with Gia and show her some love."

"Good." She wiped sleep out of my eyes and wrapped her thigh around me. "She really cares about what you think of her. She needs you more than ever right now."

"Thank you for getting her here. I appreciate you."

"You better." She punched my arm and I chuckled at her weak ass hit.

Reaching for my phone on the nightstand, I positioned it in front of us for her to peep what I was doing.

"Splurge on yourself today. On my dime." She tried to snatch my phone out of my hand, but I held her wrists together, pinning them above her head.

"I don't want your money, Grayson."

I shut her up with a sloppy, passionate kiss.

"You don't need it either, but I want you to have it," I pulled back and said.

"I love you," she whispered against my lips. "Feels surreal saying it out loud."

"Realest love I've ever felt." My hands travelled between her warm thighs. As I eased my way up, the wetness from her pussy coated my fingertips. She was always ready for me to enter her, and I didn't take that access for granted. I never would.

"Good morning, y'all," Gianna shouted from the other side of the door, followed by hard knocks. "I made breakfast. Grits. Eggs. Bacon. Maple sausages. Waffles. There's some fruit and—"

"Breakfast, Gia. We get it," I quipped.

"Come eat, ugly."

"Good morning, boo. We're coming!" Molli returned.

"Okay," Gia chimed, humming as she walked off.

"Yeah, not the way I wanted to come either," I mumbled against Molli's neck.

"You're so nasty." Molli's fine ass abandoned me and got out of bed. It took a lot of restraint not to pull her back down, spread her legs, and taste her. "Jump in the shower with me. You won't regret it." She pulled my T-shirt over her head and tossed it aside. A glimpse of her naked, stacked body had my dick so hard it ached, then she disappeared into the bathroom.

"Don't keep me waiting," she said seconds before the shower started.

It didn't make any sense how much I loved and adored that woman.

I KNEW GIANNA WOULD BE MAD AT MY NEXT MOVE, but I didn't expect her to give me the silent treatment.

After our breakfast with Molli, I took Gia to a few of her favorite boutiques downtown to shop. Shopping always solved her problems and made her feel better. I blamed our parents for that. They'd always given her whatever she wanted, but their cash flow would've halted altogether if they knew she was pregnant. All they ever asked of her was for her to focus on school. After all, they were the ones fronting the bill for her to attend college.

Now, we were at my condo, sitting in the living room on the couch across from her boyfriend, Xavier, who was sitting in my favorite chair. For twenty minutes straight, she pouted and ignored us by staring off at the wall, refusing to speak or respond to anything we said.

"Let me get this straight," she finally spoke, flipping her curls out of her face. "You invited him out here without telling me?"

Xavier could handle his own; I fucked with that about him. Though he was only twenty years old, he had his head on straight. One conversation with him was all it took for me to determine that he was raised by good people.

"I asked him if I could come here to be with you," he spoke up for himself. "Why are you running from me anyway, Gianna?" His intense stare was pinned on her. Even when he rubbed his hand over his low-cut and brushed it down his face, his eyes never left her.

Xavier had an earring with a cross on it dangling from his right ear. His jeans were too tight, and he smoothed his hands over his shirt every five minutes. I assumed he was a pretty boy ass nigga when I initially shook hands with him, but I appreciated how he stepped up to the plate regardless. He loved Gianna and his actions proved that.

"It's not like that." She sighed and dropped her head.

"Can you tell me what it's like? Because I'm right here, putting everything on hold to chase after you—"

"No one told you to do that." She folded her arms across her chest and avoided eye contact with him. "You could've stuck with your plan and went back to Houston to visit your parents' for spring break."

I wanted to tell her to grow the fuck up and talk things out with him, but I reminded myself that she was somewhat still a child. Gianna was still finding her way, and unfortunately, she didn't know how to handle shit properly.

"Aye, I'm going to run a few errands and let y'all

talk alone. I'll be back later."

"*Alone?*" Gianna asked. Her eyes widened, and Xavier side-eyed me.

"Yes. Alone." I looked her upside her head. "The damage is done. Ain't like he can get you pregnant again," I sneered. "Stay out of my damn room," I said before charging out of the front door.

Our parents, especially our father, wasn't going to take the sudden news well. But I needed Gianna to be certain of her next move before she told them she was pregnant. The first question they asked anytime we fucked up was, *"So what's your plan?"* If we didn't have a thorough answer for them, all hell broke loose.

When I got outside, I took a deep breath and tried my hardest to silence my thoughts. My little sister had always been in a rush to grow up and get out of our parent's house to do her own thing. Shit had backfired in the worst way for her, and I couldn't rescue her from this one. That realization hurt me more than anything else.

I couldn't save Gianna from her mistakes anymore, supporting her through whatever she decided to do was my only option.

Molli was right; Gianna had to figure this one out on her own.

Chapter 6

MOLLI

I tried to avoid Monika's suspicious glare, but she wouldn't let up. I searched through the rack of cocktail dresses in Neiman Marcus with her eyes drilling a hole in my face. The intensity of her stare packed a mean punch.

My older sister knew me better than anyone else did. Actually, she knew me *and* Mona better than anyone else did. She was just like our mother. Somehow, they had supernatural powers and knew everything before we found the guts to tell them.

"You want to tell me about the man from the Smokehouse," she said. "Donovan's friend or whatever." I hated how easy it was for her to figure me out. "I know you love him because I've hardly talked to you lately. You went from calling me a hundred times a day to only responding in our group chat a few times a week."

"Now, Monika. Come on." I tried to refrain from blushing, but I couldn't help it. I did love him, and I had been busy loving him, too. "I talk in the group chat all the time. Don't do that."

"Mhm." She playfully rolled her eyes while sorting through the dresses on the opposite side of the rack. "You know I'm over thirteen weeks pregnant and getting big as a house every day, yet you brought me to Neiman Marcus to taunt me with clothes I can't fit."

"No. I brought you here to buy you something nice. You won't be pregnant forever. You'll get your body back, girl."

"Molli." She rounded the rack to stand beside me. With her hand on her hip, she looked me up and down with those big brown eyes of hers. "Tell me about him."

I took a deep breath, unsure on where to start. She was there when I first laid eyes on Grayson. Mona warned me to stay away from him because he was her boyfriend's promiscuous brother/business partner, and she'd heard a lot about him and his player antics.

I saw how other women outwardly lusted over

Grayson and tried to flirt with him. Half of their business at Powell's Southern Smokehouse seemed to be women who wanted Grayson or Donovan's attention. Still, I found myself in his office, locking lips with a stranger I was attracted to like a magnet.

It'd been two months since we jumped the gun and risked it all by kissing in his office. After one kiss, he asked me out on a date and shut the Smokehouse down for us to have a private dinner. He decorated the restaurant with candles and made sure the head chef took care of us. From there, history.

We were so consistent with each other that falling in love became inevitable. It was bound to happen, and I knew it would.

"I love him, Mo," I blurted out, throwing my arms in the air for emphasis. "And I know what you're going to say—"

"That y'all are moving entirely too fast?"

"Yes, and I don't disagree with you, but—"

"It's out of your control. Your heart has decided on him, and you're in love with him."

"Okay, please stop doing that. You're driving me nuts."

"You've been nuts," she muttered and draped her arm around my shoulders. "Listen, I know you and Mona like to give me a hard time about not understanding your love lives. Y'all think I had it easy because I'm married to my high school sweetheart and blah blah. But I do understand, Mol. I understand falling in love beyond your control. I understand looking at someone and knowing they're the one. Yes, I'm hard on you and Mona sometimes, but I just want the best for my little sisters. And y'all have dealt with some shitty men in the past, so I deserve to be a little overprotective."

Tears sprang to my eyes; I didn't understand why I'd suddenly gotten emotional. Monika noticed and hugged me tightly in her arms.

"I support this love. You don't think I've noticed how much that man adds onto your happiness? Long as he keeps that up, we're good."

I whimpered as her hug got tighter by the minute. "I need to breathe to survive," I reminded her.

Releasing me from her arms, she wiped her watering eyes and swiped a stray tear from my cheek. "I only want what's best for you. You're one of the hardest working women I know. A damn good writer. Best seller, may I add?"

"Yes, you may." I bat my lashes.

"You're an amazing woman, and you deserve

better than what you've gotten in the past from men," she declared, and I nodded to agree.

"Speaking of the past." I laughed while gathering my composure. "Ever since I invited Grayson to the lounge a couple weeks ago, Kennan has been trying to slide his way back in my life. I wish he'd quit at the lounge already and work somewhere else. I love Stardust too much to stop going because of him."

"He can slide his way to the hottest, darkest part of hell."

"Mo." I gasped. It was funny hearing Monika talk like that. She prided herself on being a Christian woman who served the lord and obeyed His word to the best of her ability. Whenever she slipped up and expressed how she really felt without restrictions, I lived for it.

"Yeah, of course he wants to slide his way back in after seeing you happy with another man. Did he forget all the unnecessary bullshit he put you through while y'all were together? All the women who were calling your phone about his dusty, dirty dick—"

"What do you think about this?" I snatched a stunning aqua blue cocktail dress from the rack and shook it in front of her. Digging deep and rehashing past events about Kennan was off limits. And so was raising Monika's blood pressure while she was pregnant. "Cute, right? It's your size and it's on sale. You want it?"

Monika peered at me through slanted eyes and smiled. Her pregnancy really had her glowing. Her deep brown skin looked like it had been kissed by the sun.

"You know I do. It's my favorite color."

"Perfect." I laid it over our cart, then placed both hands on her stomach. "Let's shop for more push, snap-back gifts."

Whether she was having a boy or girl, I didn't care. Monika and her husband didn't either. They wanted to be surprised at birth by the gender. Our family simply prayed for a healthy baby.

"I'm going to be your favorite aunt," I whispered to her growing belly.

I loved Mona dearly, but she didn't stand a chance.

BACK AT HOME, GRAYSON AND GIANNA WERE missing, but I was okay with that right now.

My publisher's assistant had sent me samples of

possible covers to choose from for my next release. I flipped back and forth between the options, unable to choose one. Moments like this, I was especially grateful my sister was one of the best graphic designers I knew. Either Monika helped me choose the best one in the bunch, or she volunteered to make something better, which my publisher's assistant always approved of and fell in love with.

Monika had gotten a lot of gigs on my behalf and I was ecstatic to support her small business in any way I could.

Pacing back and forth in my living room, I studied the photos on my iPad, zooming in and tapping the screen hard while huffing every other minute. Five books in and the process of writing, completing, and preparing a novel for production never got any easier. I loved what I did, and my passion for my craft ran deep, but divine execution was a real bitch sometimes!

A bottle of Dom Perignon was screaming my name from the kitchen. I tossed my iPad on my purple, suede loveseat and headed for it, but my doorbell chimed and stopped me in my tracks. Since I wasn't expecting anyone, I dug in the back pocket of my jeans and pulled out my phone. then clicked on the Ring app to view the camera outside of my door.

A delivery man popped up on my screen. In his hands were two bunches of flowers with a straw tie wrapped around them. Sunflowers and roses mixed together was one of my favorite visuals outside of them being my favorite flowers.

Only one person knew that about me.

When we were together, Kennan used to have two bunches of the beautiful mixture delivered to me every week.

This move had him written all over it.

Stashing my phone back in my pocket, I opened the door and accepted the delivery. They were too beautiful too turn away, but I could've done without the card that read:

Seeing you again last night made me realize how much I miss you. - Kennan

The fuck was that?

Since I'd known Kennan, he'd always done the bare minimum and assumed it was enough for me. He'd had more chances with me than he deserved, and he would never receive another one.

I carried the flowers into the kitchen to throw them away, but I couldn't bring myself to do it. Despite him being a lying, disloyal asshole, the flowers were innocent and a perfect addition to the sunflowers in the big vase that were set on the middle of my center island.

Suddenly, Grayson's cologne embraced me moments before he hugged me from behind.

"What I tell you about leaving the front door unlocked?" He kissed my neck, distracting me from giving him a real answer. My eyes closed as I got lost in him. His growing dick was pressed against my ass and I immediately felt safe and content in his arms.

"What's that?" He stepped back, and my eyes shot open at the card that came attached to the flowers. "Nice flowers," he muttered, unimpressed.

"It's..." I shrugged. "It's nothing," I said, because that's exactly what it meant to be.

Nothing.

Grayson picked up the card anyway. My breathing hitched as his eyes roamed over every inch of the small, white and pink card.

"*Seeing you again last night?*" he read aloud, now looking back and forth between me and the card in his hand. "Who the fuck is Kennan, and why did he have the pleasure of seeing my woman last night?"

"Kennan is..." I sighed, already tired of thinking about him and mentioning his name. Just the thought of that man and his bullshit exhausted me. "Nobody," I finished and snatched the card from his hand. After ripping it into small shreds, I threw the pieces in the trash.

"I hung out with Jana at the lounge last night and he was the bouncer for the night," I explained. "He tried to ask me how I was and get a conversation going but I ignored him."

"Oh. That nigga." Grayson chuckled, an amused smile taking over his handsome face. "He didn't have that energy when he saw us there together a while back."

"He didn't have that energy until he saw me with someone else."

"You disappointed about that?"

"What? No. I'm a little aggravated and offended by it, but it is what it is. Everything happened the way it was supposed to," I said, walking into his arms.

Grayson peered down into my eyes, studying them for the truth. When he was finished over analyzing them, he gripped my chin and said, " I trust you."

"Good. You should. Hurting you is the last thing I ever want to do."

"Do you trust me?" he asked, and I hesitated to answer.

I did trust him! Or, maybe, I wanted to trust him so badly that I convinced myself I did. Now that he'd questioned me about it, I wondered if I truly did. I understood I couldn't love him beyond a shadow of a doubt if I didn't trust him, so I needed to trust him.

"I don't like that answer," he said, calling out my silence. No answer was an answer to him.

I wasn't pretending to be distracted by his light brown eyes, I really was.

His flawless, chocolate skin.

Pearly white teeth.

Long bowlegs.

The total package of him was distracting. Grayson was the epitome of a fine, smooth, breathtaking man, and I wanted to trust him beyond a shadow of a doubt. I needed to.

"I'm all in with you, Grayson. We haven't confirmed our relationship or thrown a title on it and I don't really care about that. But I'm all in with you. Sometimes I wonder if you're all in with me, too."

"M. Hill," he murmured and tucked a thick strand of my hair behind my ear. Hearing him call me by my pen name made me giggle. "You don't have to wonder." Grayson towered over me and shook his head. A smile slowly curled his lips. "I haven't looked at a fat ass since I laid eyes on yours." He cupped my face.

"Grayson!" I swatted his hand away from my face and he brought it right back, caressing my cheek this time.

"Let's confirm what this is right now. Let's put a title on us."

"I don't want you to take this the wrong way, but my sister told me about you before we met. She told me you date a lot of women."

"Damn, so Mona been throwing dirt on my name? I should've known."

"It's not like that," I said. "But she's my sister. She's been with Donovan for a while, so she knows a little bit about you. You're around them a lot."

"Molli, let me bring you up to date." He lifted me in his arms, sitting me on the edge of the island. Standing between my thighs, he grabbed my hands, holding onto them as he continued. "I used to date a lot of women. I was single and uninterested in taking anyone serious. My main excuse was that I was focused on expanding our business at the

Smokehouse. Being committed to one woman was an effort I wasn't ready to give."

"I see..." I whispered.

"Then, I saw you. I met you. I jumped the gun by pulling you into my office and kissing you. Shit was so unexpected that it caught even me off guard. I been putting in the effort, Mol. I'm already committed. There's no one else. Not anymore, and not ever again if you'll trust me to love and take care of you."

Draping my arms over his shoulders, I pulled him into a hug and laid my head close to his neck. His masculine, cocoa bean scent made me feel warm inside.

"I've been fucked over, Grayson. Cheated on. Manipulated. Taken advantage of for having a forgiving heart and being stupid at the same time." I laughed at myself. I couldn't blame anyone but myself for the degrading things I'd accepted in past relationships. I didn't love myself enough back then. Now, I loved and adored myself too much to put up with less than I deserved.

"And I know none of that has anything to do with you, and I'll never blame you for someone else's mistakes or take anything out on you. But I need to know that you're all in with no outside attachments. I can't risk my peace being disturbed again by a man who has one foot in and one foot out. I don't want stick figures keyed into the side of my car anymore by women who feel they're in competition with me over my man," I finished.

"He wasn't running his ship right," Grayson said.

I snapped my neck at him so hard that my head almost rolled off of it and onto the floor.

"Don't play with me."

"I told you what I used to do." He wrapped his hand around my neck, smiling as he rubbed his thumb over my sensitive spot. "Then I told you what I want to do. With you. Did you miss that? Loving and taking care of you doesn't come with outside attachments that will fuck us over," he explained. "I'm thirty-two and—"

"And because of your age you think you should settle down now?" I held back from scoffing. I despised when people based their decisions on their age and what they felt they should've been doing because of it.

"I was going to say I'm finding my way. Coming into my own. I'm more of a man now, one who no longer wants to test the waters or waste time. A grown ass man who wants to love you and you only," he said. "What's up with you today?" He searched my eyes for answers, clearly amused at my attitude from the grin plastered on his face.

"I'm sorry." I sighed. "It's just...I love you. More than I loved him, and you have no idea what I accepted because of my love for him."

"It's all good, baby. You're not going to lose yourself in me, I won't let you."

Tracing his bottom lip with my index finger, I blushed at the plumpness of them. Pressed against mine, they felt magical to me, but when they were flowing across my skin, they felt perfect.

He grabbed and kissed the top of my hand. "I love you too."

I reeled him in by wrapping my thighs around his waist, then regretted it when he whisked me around the kitchen in circles.

"Grayson!" I squealed until he placed my back against the wall.

"So, tell me. What's up with me and you, beautiful?"

"You been my man since our first kiss. Act like you know," I quipped, panting as he unbuttoned my jeans while kissing my breath away.

"I don't have hours to play with you," I spoke

through moans. "I have emails to respond to and graphics to decide on for my novel."

"And I'm supposed to be on my way to Toledo to check out a new lot for our third Smokehouse location. I drove to you instead."

"Damn," I whispered against his lips, then sucked his bottom lip into my mouth. "I think I might have a few hours to spare after all."

The way he prioritized me turned me on.

"I need you to do something for me," he said, peeling my jeans down to my ankles.

In my head I'd shouted, *anything for you*, but the words wouldn't emit. I was too busy watching his every move, anxious for whatever came next.

Releasing his hard dick from his pants, he stroked it with his free hand, then lowered me on the wall to rub it against my clit.

I knew what he needed. And I wanted to hear his deep voice say it.

"Come on my dick." He eased inside the pussy that was always wet and ready for him, and my eyes rolled into the back of my head.

"Grayson, please," I whimpered.

The slight hook in his dick was lethal. It gravitated to my G-spot with purpose to drive me crazier over him. "Please," I whispered again, melting into him.

"Deeper." I directed him deeper when I didn't mean it—when I was already struggling to take the dick that he was giving me. A charm from my ankle bracelet tapped his ear as he lifted my leg over his shoulder.

I'd never known myself to be flexible, but there was no level to what I could do with or for him. Grayson was amused at my eyes crossing. My mouth was wide open as he made me take every inch he had to offer.

"Look at me," he said, our eyes connecting immediately. He thrusted into me with purpose to take my soul, and I gazed into his light brown eyes, trying my hardest to not only keep them straight, but open.

"Fuck." He slapped his hand on the wall beside me. "Look how you're creaming all on this dick." We both looked down to enjoy the view. In awe, I whimpered as I watched him ease inside and out of me.

Catching me off guard, he flipped me into a handstand. His grip on me was firm as he slapped my ass, deeply groaning through the immense pleasure.

"Yes, baby." I lifted one of my arms to rub his buff chest. "Right there. Oh my God! Right there." I tried my best to take it for him, but Grayson wasn't playing fair. He demanded I came on his dick, then teased my asshole with his thumb.

"You got that for me?" he asked.

"Yes!" I screamed, squirting on his dick as my body trembled.

He caught me in his arms before my body weakened and hit the ground. Together, we dropped to the cold tile floor, panting in each other's arms.

Grayson belonged exactly where he was right now. With me.

"Let me take you on a date," he blurted and scooped me into an embrace. Standing from the floor, he threw me over his shoulder like I was a weightless rag doll and carried me into my bedroom.

"A date? It's getting late."

"So what, grandma." He tossed me onto the middle of my bed. "Get dressed."

"Are you for real right now? After that workout you just put me through?"

"We need to do something to celebrate you turning in your book," he said while sorting through his clothing in a drawer that neither of us directly spoke about. I didn't know when it exactly happened during the two months we'd been dating, but we'd gotten really comfortable in each other's homes. "And wear something normal. Something casual. Last time we went out people were distracted by that bright ass glitter, sequin blouse you had on."

"Hey!" I chucked a pillow at him and it bounced off of his shoulder. He didn't even flinch. "You said I looked beautiful in that."

"You did, baby. That's a given. But that shit was loud."

"Shut up! Monika bought me that shirt."

"That's the oldest one, right?" He rose an eyebrow and I nodded. "That explains it," he mumbled. "Come shower. We're late meeting up with Don and Mona." He disappeared into the bathroom as I side-eyed the threshold.

"As in my sister?" I shouted behind him.

"Who else?" He kissed his teeth. "Woman, get yo' ass in here!" he started the shower, shouting over the powerful jets.

Stripping quickly, I rushed into the bathroom to join him. Grayson was always up to something that swooned me. I couldn't wait to find out what it was this time.

———————

"YOU CAN OPEN YOUR EYES NOW," GRAYSON SAID. His Escalade hadn't stopped yet, but I opened my eyes to him pulling into an available parking spot close to the front entrance of the building.

I covered my mouth and burst into laughter. "Main Event!?"

"Main Event," he confirmed.

Main Event was a huge building of fun and one of my favorite places to hang out at. They had bowling alleys, video games, laser tag, karaoke, and the list continued.

My sisters and I were obsessed with the place when we were teenagers. And Mona and I weren't ashamed that our obsession had carried on into our adulthood.

"What made you... I mean—"

"You always talk my head off about your sisters and how y'all used to have the best time here," he said. Reaching for my hand, he kissed the top of it and expressed, "You can't work your ass off and not enjoy yourself. I know you talk about how hard I work all the time, but at least I have poker night with the boys once a week. Just visiting your sisters' cribs is not enough. I want you to have the time of your life like you used to," he expressed. "With the help of Don, I reached out and invited your sisters. I forgot Monika was pregnant, though. She wasn't feeling up for it."

"Oh, Grayson." I blushed and climbed over the middle console to straddle his lap. "You're so sweet to me. And trust me, pregnant or not, Monika wouldn't have been up for it." I snickered.

"Yeah, I want all that. What else am I to you?"

"Don't push it." I kissed his cheek, looping my arms around his neck. "But you're everything," I whispered in his ear. "In a short time, you've become everything to me."

"After I went out of my way to search for you on Facebook because you ran from me after our first kiss, I knew you would become everything to me, too."

"In my defense, people don't just introduce themselves to others and then kiss right after."

"You kissed me first, though."

"I did not!"

"You walked into my office, in my restaurant,

claiming you were looking for your sister and kissed me first."

"That's not how it happened." I folded my arms across my chest. In reality, that was exactly how it happened. Well, the first part of what he said was how it happened. As for our kiss, our lips and moves were in sync. Our heads nearly banged into each other's as we moved in closer for that kiss.

Grayson's phone sounded and interrupted our debate. He pulled it from his pocket and chuckled at the screen. "It's Don. He says Mona keeps asking him where I'm at with her sister," he said. "Damn. We're only ten minutes late."

I opened his door, and he held onto my hand as I stepped out. "We're overprotective of each other."

"You think?"

"Come on." I laughed and tugged at his arm.

I couldn't wait to beat all their asses in laser tag.

Chapter 7

GRAYSON

Carrying Molli into her bedroom, I laid her on the bed and chuckled in her ear. "You want mercy or dick tonight?" I asked.

"Both." She used all her strength to flip us over. Throwing her hair over her shoulder, she gyrated her hips. Molli closed her eyes while fluffing her fingers through her hair, and I could tell she was riding my dick to a slow beat in her head.

I leaned up and lifted her shirt over her head, slinging it across the room.

Her cleavage looked beautiful in her purple lace bra. I kissed the top of her breasts as I unhooked it and tossed it aside.

"These muthafuckas right here," I said, burying my face into them. She reminded me of butter pecan at all times. To me, that was her flavor. On top of that, she always smelled like vanilla bean. I was starting to think I was addicted to everything about her. She giggled and moaned while I motorboated and caressed them. My mouth watered at the sight of her hard nipples. They poked out and teased me relentlessly. I slapped her hand away when she tried to play with them.

"I got that," I said, covering her right nipple with my mouth. She bounced up and down faster; her head tilted back as I swirled my tongue around her nipple.

"This my dick," she whispered in my ear.

"Mhm." I smiled and slapped her ass. I'd taught her well. "Get this dick, baby. You know it's yours."

Her moans got louder, and her thighs trembled, but she knew better than to tap out on me. She handled her first orgasm like a champ, her eyes watering through the pleasure.

After pushing me onto my back, she held onto the top of the headboard, riding me in a slow, sensual rhythm. Our eyes latched onto each other's, neither of us blinking as we climaxed together.

Flipping her onto her back, I kissed her neck, then took a deep breath in her ear. "I'm not done with you," I said.

I didn't believe I would ever be.

"Baby," she moaned, gripping my wrist to stop my next move. "It's too—"

"Don't give out on me just yet," I murmured, spreading her wet pussy lips and taking in the view.

I tapped her clit two times, circling the sensitive bud with the pad of my thumb. Her body twitched beneath me, and I smirked. Molli was spent, but I wouldn't let her rest until I got my fill of her. "On your stomach," I demanded.

She flipped over, and I grabbed a pillow, placing it under her body so that she was slightly elevated. I glanced up and found her peering at me over her shoulder.

"Relax, baby," I said, gripping both of her ass cheeks and spreading them. Not wasting any time, I buried my face between her supple skin and dragged my tongue from her pussy to her ass.

"Ooh," she moaned, shaking on contact. "Yes!" I continued to feast and get my fix until she let out a strangled cry and tried escaping my hold.

Before I could release her, I lapped up her

essence, letting it coat my tongue before letting up. As always, she tasted fucking divine.

Her body sagged against the mattress, but I couldn't let Molli get too comfortable. In one swift motion, I pushed my way inside of her.

"Fuck!" we cursed in unison. The first stroke was always the most intense. It almost broke me down, but I maintained my stamina.

"I-I can't," she cried.

I pressed against her back and whispered into her ear, "Yes, you can, baby." As I slowly stroked her tight walls, Molli's soft whimpers grew louder. "That's right give me one more. I know you got it in you," I coached her. "Give me what I want."

"Oh my—"

"Mmhm," I hummed, slamming into her with our bodies still pressed together. "There you go." I slipped an arm beneath her, needing to feel closer. Needing to stay connected. "Pussy, so damn good, woman."

"Yours," she croaked. I smiled into her neck and lifted my pelvis, jerking back and then forward again. "Again. That's my girl."

Over and over, I pounded into her from behind. When Molli's breathing picked up, and her loud moans returned to low murmurs of pleasure, I knew she was close. I was so damn close, too. So, I pressed my thumb into her ass and held it there. That sent my baby over the edge, and I released right behind her.

Just when she thought I was going to give her a break, I eased out of her to taste her. Her sheets were soaked, and I thrived off that. She had the juiciest pussy I'd ever had. The sweetest pussy that had me lying on my stomach like a sniper while I admired it.

I vibrated my tongue around her clit, pausing every ten seconds to smile at her dripping wet, pulsating pussy. Softly, Molli repeatedly moaned my name.

"Why are you fucking me like this?" She asked, and I chuckled. It amused me every time she asked me that.

Molli deserved endless pleasure, and I planned on catering to her every need.

"Last one and I'll give you a break," I promised, then laid beside her and positioned her on my face. She hung onto the headboard as she whined her hips. Her thighs trembled over me while I massaged and spread her ass cheeks. Now wasn't the time to latch onto her clit, so I didn't. She was in control of riding my tongue and brushing her sensitive clit across my lips.

"Grayson. Oh God. I—" A powerful orgasm made her collapse on my face. Her thighs damn near smothered me and I welcomed that fate.

"Good girl." I kissed her pussy a final time, slapping her ass before allowing her to roll over onto her back and catch her breath.

I wasn't ashamed to admit that woman had me, a grown ass man, weak in the knees. I stumbled out of bed to cop a warm rag for the rounds I put her through.

Soon as I walked out of her master bathroom, I heard her light snores. Molli's legs were wide open as she moaned my name in her sleep.

"I love you, Grayson. Thank you for tonight," she stirred in her sleep and said.

I gently wiped her fat, sensitive pussy and whispered, "I love you too beautiful."

If there was another word to use, one deeper or beyond love, I would've recited it to her beautiful ass every chance I got. For now, I was forced to settle for telling her I loved her.

Molli owned my heart and this dick.

I HESITATED TO TURN THE DOORKNOB TO MY OWN crib.

When I left earlier, Gianna was being a brat and Xavier was working overtime trying to get through to her. I'd been gone all day and I wasn't surprised I hadn't received a call or text from her. Xavier had her occupied. She could try fronting on him in front of me all she wanted to, but her love for him was evident. She probably broke down and submitted to him as soon as I left them alone in my condo. The thought of that irritated me, but I understood she was an adult now and I had to respect that.

I *tried* to respect that.

Facing my reality, I opened the door and smelled bacon... again. She must've been craving it or something. This was twice in one day for her.

In the kitchen, Gianna was sitting on the countertop with Xavier standing between her legs. I thought about lunging at him, KO'ing his ass, then stomping his face in. He wasn't a bad dude, but Gianna was my little sister. Nobody deserved her and I would always believe that.

Clearing my throat, I leaned against the doorway, glaring at them. Xavier jumped back as Gianna hopped down and stood next to him.

"I take it y'all got something solved today," I

said. Gianna fluffed her fingers through her curls and reached for his hand with her free hand. She looped her fingers through his and smiled up at him.

"We decided we're not keeping it."

"Not keeping it as in?" I straightened my posture and maintained my straight face. No, I wasn't happy she'd gotten pregnant during her freshman year in college. But the thought of being an uncle excited me. Regardless of how pissed I was at her carelessness, I couldn't control that feeling.

"I've scheduled an abortion. It's in a few days, and back in Miami at my physician's office. We're leaving tomorrow afternoon to head back to campus."

"Gianna." I sighed, brushing my hand down my face. "Are you sure you—"

"Yes, we're sure," she cut me off and nodded.

"I'm not asking about y'all as a collective. I'm asking about you!" I unintentionally shouted. "This is your body, your decision and your life," I said. "Xavier, my bad, man. I'm not trying to shit on you or disregard how you feel. I know you should have a say in this, but she'll have to physically and mentally live with this decision."

"Grayson! Stop it," she whispered, her eyes pleading for me to stop before I took it any further.

"Are you sure, Gianna?! Because if you're not sure, we can figure this shit out. We'll deal with Mom and Dad later and figure this shit out, yo."

"Grayson, I'm sure, okay! Just drop it already. We've made a decision. Together. And that's what I'm going to do. It's what I want to do!" Tears fell from her eyes and fucked me up. She pulled Xavier out of the kitchen. "Xavier is taking me to Molli's house to get my things. I'm staying downtown at the Hilton with him tonight," she spoke behind her shoulder.

I opened my mouth to call out to her. To stop her and tell them to at least use my crib for the night. But I was too tired to object.

I'd been bailing my little sister out of her fuckups since she was sixteen years old. I kept her darkest secrets from our parents, and I was her best friend through every adversity she endured, whether it was inevitable or her fault. There had never been a time I dropped the ball on her or wasn't there for her.

Getting this shit through my head was hard. I didn't want to accept that she was pregnant and facing one of the toughest decisions of her life.

I didn't want to accept that I couldn't save her from everything. And I damn sure didn't want to accept that her boyfriend had stepped in and taken my little sister from me.

I knew I couldn't save her from everything, but I couldn't stop trying to.

Chapter 8
MOLLI

"Give me a break. We've been at this all morning." I plopped down onto the couch and reached for my tall wine glass of Dom Perignon "It's damn near lunch time."

Monika slapped my hand down and moved the glass away from me. She kept pacing back and forth in the living room and it was flaring my damn anxiety.

"You need to choose a cover, Molli. You always wait last minute to do these things, then you end up complaining that you didn't promote enough and blah blah." She rubbed her stomach while she ranted, and that made me smile. I couldn't help but daydream about how good of a mother she was going to be.

"*And blah blah*? Really?" I folded my arms across my chest and cut my eyes at her.

"Now isn't the time to be a spoiled brat." She grabbed a sugar cookie from the coffee table in front of the couch and bit a chunk from it. "The options are laid out in front of you." She pointed at the print outs of covers on the coffee table. The three options taunted me. I loved each of them equally.

"Because of your title, I think you should go with option B." She pulled a laser pointer from a pocket on her dress and my eyes widened.

"When did you start wearing dresses with pockets on them?"

"Since I got pregnant and comfortability became a priority for me. Are you judging me? Because me, my dress, and our pockets can go." She put her hand on her hip and side-eyed me. "Yes, there's two of them on here."

Looking at Monika was like looking at an uptight version of myself. When she didn't have a scowl on her face and her features were soft, she could've been mistaken for my dark-skinned twin.

Just like Mona, she'd gotten her beautiful skin from our mother, along with her long legs that I was envious of. Sometimes it sucked being the shortest sister.

"Earth to Molli." Monika snapped her fingers in my face. "You know what, here." She picked up my glass of Dom and handed it to me. "This seems to be the only way you can focus today."

"Thank you," I accepted the glass with a smile. "Option B, it is."

"Are you just saying that because I made it?"

"Are you saying it's the better option because you made it?"

"No."

"Great. Then it's a no for me, too. Option B, it is," I said. "Thank you for your help."

"I don't know how I deal with you." She grabbed another cookie before plopping down on the other end of the couch. "Mona said she's on the way." She read a text from her phone and tossed it onto the middle cushion.

I picked it up and read the part of Mona's message that she left out, *"Got caught up with Donovan."*

"You knew that already. I didn't have to read that part to you." Monika grabbed the remote from the glass top coffee table and turned on Lifetime Movie Network.

"She's in love. Stop hating."

"You're both in love. I'm not hating. I'm happy for y'all. I like Donovan and Grayson."

"Who are you and what have you done with my sister?"

"Shut up." She snickered. "So far, they seem like good, respectable men and I'm happy about that. Y'all deserve that. It's nice that they are practically brothers, too. I mean, I tried to hook y'all up with Joe's brothers, but whatever. We could've been going on big family trips and—"

"You tried to hook us up with Joe's ugly, nerdy brothers," I corrected her.

"What are you trying to say about Joe? His brothers definitely favor him."

Saved by the doorbell, I jumped up from the couch and made a beeline toward the front door. Molli must've forgotten her spare key, or else she would've walked right into my house like it belonged to her. We didn't live more than a half hour from each other, but with the way she turned curbs on two wheels in her Volkswagen, it took her no time at all to arrive at my place whenever she advised me that she was on the way.

I unlocked the door and swung it open, expecting to see Mona, but it wasn't her. Gianna was standing on my doorstep with tears in her eyes. An oversized, black sweatshirt hung past her knees, and she had on pink bunny slippers like she'd just gotten out of bed. Her cheeks were flushed, and though the hood part of the sweatshirt covered her head, I could tell her curls were untamed underneath it.

"Hey." She sniffled. "I'm just here to get my things out the guest room."

"Y-yeah, of course." I stood aside and motioned for her to come inside. "Are you okay?" I shouldn't have asked that question. It was obvious she wasn't okay. She looked like she was due to go berserk at any moment.

Gianna shook her head slowly and then vigorously. Thirty seconds later, she broke down and I pulled her into my arms.

Monika appeared in the threshold of the living room and stared at us. I nodded to confirm her assumption. There wasn't much I didn't tell my sisters. When we weren't together to discuss things going on in our lives, our group chat did the job.

Mona and Monika learned about Gianna from the moment she wrote me on Facebook and threatened me not to hurt her brother. They knew about her pregnancy, and after my last, short phone call with a distraught Grayson this morning, they knew she'd decided on an abortion.

The sadness in his tone while he explained their last conversation to me tore me to pieces. It worried me that I hadn't heard from him since then. My calls and texts went unanswered, but I didn't take it personal. I respected his space. However, I missed him.

I missed him so much that it physically hurt. Staying busy all morning was the only thing keeping me sane.

"You should come sit down and relax for a minute," Monika suggested, and Gianna's head shot up from my shoulder as her eyes darted in Monika's direction.

"That's my sister, Monika. It's okay," I assured her.

"I-I told my boyfriend I would be back soon and—"

"Oh, he can wait, sweetheart. You don't need to get back on the road like that."

"She doesn't know how to take no for an answer," I whispered to Gianna, leading her into the living room and rubbing her back.

"Did you eat anything today?" Monika asked. "I could fix you something." She patted the couch for

Gianna to take a seat, then rushed into the kitchen and returned with a bottle of water and a can of ginger-ale.

"Oh God, Monika." I sighed, holding back from laughing. She couldn't help herself. She was nurturing and overbearing by nature. She was our mother through and through.

"I don't really have an appetite," Gianna said, speaking barely above a whisper.

"That doesn't mean you shouldn't try eating a little something." Monika pushed the plate of sugar cookies closer to the edge of the table.

"Mo." I looked in her eyes and shook my head.

"Okay," she surrendered and sat on the other side of Gianna.

"Thank you," Gianna said as she twisted the cap to the water bottle open and took a small sip. Her hands trembled and faint whimpers emitted from her. She was trying to hold back from breaking down again, and I hoped like hell she didn't. I felt for her, and my eyes were watering because of it.

"Do you want to talk about it?" Monika asked. Her eyes were watering too, and that shocked me.

"You wouldn't understand," Gianna mumbled, then cleared her throat.

"Try me," Monika challenged her, and my eyebrow immediately rose. Because she knew Gianna's dilemma already, her response caught me off guard.

Of course, we could emphasize with Gianna, but could we truly understand what she was going through if we hadn't been through it ourselves?

"I want an abortion," Gianna started, wiping tears from her eyes. "I don't want kids right now." She dropped her head and twiddled her thumbs. "But I feel so guilty. It's eating me alive and I haven't even done it yet."

While Gianna had our undivided attention, Mona arrived and walked into the living room. "What's going on?" she mouthed, confusion slanting her eyes and scrunching her nose like she was having trouble seeing. She sat across from us in the beanbag lounger in the corner.

"The guilt you feel right now is only the beginning," Monika said, grabbing Gianna's hand. "If you get the procedure, it gets worse. The guilt will destroy you if you let it. You have to be sure this is what you really want before you do it, because if you have any doubts…" Monika paused as tears fell from her eyes and streamed down her cheeks.

"You had an abortion before?" Gianna whispered, looking up at Monika.

Monika nodded. "When I was eighteen."

"What!?" Mona and I shouted in unison.

"You did what?" Mona leaned forward in her seat, staring at Monika in horror.

"Why are we just now hearing about this?" I asked. For reasons I couldn't fully explain or understand, I got mad, then sad. Actually, I was a mixture of many emotions. My sister had gone through something that extreme, at eighteen-years-old, and I never knew about it. The realization broke my heart and shocked me at once.

"No one knew but Mom and Joe," Monika said, looking back and forth from me and Mona. In our eyes, she was the innocent sister—our older Christian sister who praised God and tried her hardest to live by the Bible's ten commandments. Lo and behold, she was just as flawed as the rest of us. I just wished we knew; I wished we could've been there for her.

"Mol, please don't." Monika sighed as I covered my face.

Mona read my thoughts when she said, "I thought there weren't any secrets between us. Why didn't you tell us or let us be there for you?"

"I'm the oldest. Y'all have always looked up to me and I'm supposed to be a positive example for you two. That's what Mom and Dad used to tell me every day. I was embarrassed. Joe and I jumped the gun and didn't protect ourselves on prom night. Only took one time."

"Just fertile and ovulating on prom night," I whispered to myself, shaking my head.

"I was embarrassed," Monika continued. "And y'all were there for me without even knowing it. Around that time, I pretended I had a terrible stomach bug and y'all took care of me."

"Oh my God, I think I remember that," Mona said.

"How old are you now? Do you still feel guilty?"

"Almost thirty-three and no. I still get sad over it sometimes. It randomly hits me and affects my mood when I least expect it. But I don't allow guilt to take over anymore. My husband and I weren't ready for children at that time, and now we are," she explained and rubbed her stomach. Gianna looked up at her and managed a smile. "We had trouble conceiving for a while, and for a long time I thought it was God punishing me for having an abortion. I'm thankful we got a second chance, but,

Gianna, sweetheart, you have to be sure this is what you want to do.

You'll go through the motions, but as long as you're sure, you'll get them through without losing yourself in the process. Put aside what everyone else may say or think about your decision, because at the end of the day, this is your life, and you'll have to battle the demons that may come from it, you understand what I mean?"

"I think so." Gianna nodded slowly and released Monika's hand. She shocked us all when she wrapped her arms around Monika and wept. "Thank you so much."

Monika hesitated for a few seconds before embracing Gianna in her arms. Together they wept as Mona and I stared at them and tried to balance the energy in the room by being strong.

"Group hug please." Mona said, standing from the beanbag chair. I followed suit and held my hand out for hers, waiting for Monika and Gianna to stand and join us.

I wasn't sure how Gianna expected her day to go when she woke up this morning, but I was thankful me and my sisters got the chance to love on and pray for her before she headed back to Miami.

For once, I responded to work emails on my iPad from the living room instead of my office. On the Alexa speaker in the background, Jhene Aiko harmonized about good dick that made her soul smile. I related to the lyrics wholeheartedly.

I stared at my phone every other minute. Grayson still hadn't returned my calls or texts from earlier, and I was racking my brain over his current state of mind.

Gianna had gotten all her things and left to return to the hotel with her boyfriend four hours ago. She wanted to talk to Grayson again before she left, but neither of us could reach him.

Eventually, I had Mona find out the scoop on his whereabouts from Donovan. He was attending poker night with his boys, so I popped a bag of popcorn, poured a glass of Dom, and worked from the living room while looking over at my phone every other minute. When he finally reached out to me, I planned on jumping at the opportunity to be there for him.

I leaped from the couch, nearly knocking over my bowl of caramel popcorn when the doorbell rang.

"Alexa, turn off music," I shouted over my shoulder, darting to the front door.

I stood on my toes to look out the peephole. Donovan and Grayson were outside of my door. Donovan held Grayson upright as Grayson tripped over his own feet. He wobbled like he was going to tip over at any minute. I'd never seen him drunk or off his game before.

"Hey." I opened the door and extended my hand for his. Grayson grabbed onto it quickly, squeezing my hand in his. In his other hand was an unopened bottle of water.

"Look at her fine ass, Don. Bad as fuck, isn't she? All that hair on her head is hers. There's no braids under that wild bird's nest." His words slurred and he shouted like we were across the street instead of standing close by him. Grayson's breath reeked of whiskey.

"Oh my God," I mumbled and smoothed my hand over my messy bun.

"I wasn't going to bring him here like this but he damn near threatened to kill me if I didn't," Donovan explained.

"It's okay. Thank you for bringing him here."

"If he wakes up and doesn't remember shit, let him know his car is at my place."

"Okay," I said, thanking him once more. "Get home safe. Have a good night." I pulled Grayson inside with me as Donovan threw his hand up and started for his car. Tugging him along felt harder than usual tonight. His dark Nike T-shirt was drenched with sweat and he only had socks on his feet; his shoes were missing.

"You 'bout to go to your girl crib and tear that ass up ain't you? I feel you, my G. Hit my line later boy." He shouted behind Donovan.

"Grayson." I covered his mouth. "Stop shouting and come inside."

Locking us inside, I pulled him into my bedroom and pushed him down on the bed. "Don't move, okay! I'm going to start a shower for you. Drink some of your water."

"Damn, woman." He sat up and licked his lips, looking me up and down. "That ass poking in them shorts." He whistled.

"Don't move," I said. "Just give me one second." Rushing into the bathroom, I started a cool shower for him. Turning back for him, I bumped into his chest and gasped. Grayson stood in the threshold, chuckling and trying to drink water that was spilling down his chin and onto the carpet.

"Didn't I tell you not to move?" I sighed.

"Aye, why you answer the door with those little ass shorts on? I don't want people seeing what's mine like that." He reeled me into his arms and slapped my ass.

Prying the bottle of water from his hands, I fought hard to undress him, then guided him inside of the sliding door shower.

He licked his lips and laughed as I lathered the loofah sponge with soap to bathe him. "If you wanted to see this dick, that's all you had to say." Grayson lifted me off my feet and whisked me into the spacious shower. I shrieked as the cool water drenched me.

"Grayson!" I punched his arm, but he wasn't fazed. His drunk ass was amused and had the nerve to help me out my tank top and shorts while he laughed. "Why'd you drink so much? Did the loser have to take shots or something?"

"That's not how the game works, baby. We play with real money, and I don't lose."

I rolled my eyes. "Yeah, okay." I washed his chest, then repositioned us by turning him toward the water.

Suddenly, a tear trailed down Grayson's cheek. I would've assumed it was water from the shower head if I were rinsing him off, but we hadn't reached that step yet.

"Wh-what's wrong? Are you in pain? What hap--" He tried dropping his head, but I refused to let him. Cupping his face, I held his head up and looked into his sad eyes. The pain in them made my heart race. "Grayson what is it? You can tell me anything. I'm here for you."

Taking a step back, he closed his eyes and let the water fall over him. Once the water impacted him, his face softened. He looked at peace, and even if it only lasted for a moment, I wanted him to enjoy it.

Rubbing the loofah over his stomach, I continued to wash him, hoping the sensation of the cool water sobered him up and helped him feel better soon.

Neither of us spoke during the rest of our shower or while we brushed our teeth afterward.

I helped him dry off and blow dried his beard after tackling and styling my damp mane into two braids.

I pulled the comforter back for him to get into bed. Though he obliged and laid down, he brought me down with him.

Grayson traced his thumb over my eyebrows

and smiled. The pain in his eyes that made my heart race earlier was still there. I prayed for it to vanish.

"That abortion shit fucks my head up," he whispered and embraced me in his arms. I laid my head on his shoulder, waiting patiently for him to say more. He paused for a few minutes before explaining himself. "Xavier doesn't want her to get one. He loves her, so he's down for whatever makes her happy. I was him. Except I was twenty-five and in love with a selfish woman who didn't even have the decency or respect to tell me she was aborting our child."

I lifted my head, and our eyes instantly met. If I could've meshed my naked body into his to get closer to him, I would've.

"One day she was pregnant and the next day she wasn't. Worst part about it, I probably wouldn't have fought her on her decision. Just like Xavier isn't fighting Gianna about it. He feels like it's out of his control. I know that feeling," he said. "I feel like a fucking hypocrite for counting him out earlier. I made it seem like his decision didn't matter. I still remember how it felt when I realized my decision didn't matter. Why did I do that to him?"

"I-I'm so sorry. Does Gianna know? I mean..." At a loss for words, I shook my head in disbelief.

What was I supposed to say to him?

"No."

"Does anyone know?" I whispered, gliding my index finger down his nose.

He swallowed hard and said, "I just told you."

"What happened after she..." I stopped speaking and sighed. It felt even heavier trying to repeat it out loud.

"We graduated from college and she accepted a job offer out of state. Her career came first to her. I didn't trip about it because I knew things would never be the same between us. We both knew."

"I don't know what to say," I admitted.

"You don't need to say anything." He cuddled me in his strong arms.

"Are you going to tell Gianna?"

"No. I'm not trying to guilt trip or convince her there's another way. I just realize why her decision affects me so much."

"I understand what you mean," I said and closed my eyes. When I opened them again, he was still staring at me while deep in thought. "I had a miscarriage a couple years ago," I blurted out. "Since we're trauma bonding and all," I mumbled, failing to be sarcastic like I intended to be. It was the first time I'd said it out loud and it almost broke me down. "I never told anyone about it. After I went to the hospital and they explained what was happening to me, I convinced myself it was for the best and forced myself to move on from it."

"Is that what you believe? That it was for the best." He pushed one of my braids behind my shoulder.

"I do. You think that's fucked up, don't you?"

"A miscarriage is out of your control." He gripped my chin, keeping my head up and our eye contact consistent. "Why are you questioning if it's fucked up? There's nothing you could've done to prevent it, Molli. You know that, right?"

Something about his deep voice being softer than I'd ever heard it brought on the water works. I tried to remove myself from his lap, but he refused to let me go.

"Don't go anywhere," he said, pressing his lips against mine. "I got you." Grayson wiped my eyes. "This happened with your ex, Kegel?"

"Yes." I burst out laughing and closed my eyes to mask my tears. "With *Kegel*," I whispered.

"I'm sorry that happened to you." He kissed my bottom lip. "You want to know what I think?"

"I always do."

"I think it wasn't time for you to become a mother yet," he simply said. "God's plan."

"I think you're right."

"Just like it wasn't my time to become a father. We weren't with the right people, we weren't ready, and it just wasn't our time to be parents," he finished and winced, massaging his temples.

"I'll be right back. I'm going to get you something for that." I escaped his arms before he tried holding me captive on his lap.

Returning with a bottle of water, Gatorade, and a few Tylenol capsules, I stood by his side of the bed. "Did you eat?"

"Yeah, Don ordered a lot of food tonight. He loves acting like he's a better host than everyone else when Poker night is at his crib," he said. "Have you seen my phone?" He looked from the nightstand on my side of the bed to his. "I think they're in the pocket of my pants. I need to check on my parents—"

"You can check on them in the morning," I said, pushing him flat on his back when he tried to sit up. "It's admirable how you look after everyone. I love that about you. But tonight, I'm looking after you." I cut off the lamp on the nightstand next to his side of the bed, then cuddled him in my arms.

Grayson held me every chance he got. Tonight, I wanted to return the favor. Gianna's sudden circumstance had led us here. Without it, I wondered if we would've ever disclosed our past situations on almost becoming parents.

Our warm, naked bodies set the bed ablaze. Our hands roamed each other's bodies, and we were content leaving it there. Experiencing Grayson deeply inside of me was one of my guilty pleasures —a pleasure I couldn't get enough of. But lying beside him tonight was enough, too.

In all, being loved by him was more than enough.

Chapter 9

GRAYSON

I wanted to wake her up like this every morning. With my tongue circling her clit as I hugged her thighs and trapped her on my face.

She moved her hips to guide me to her spot, as if I didn't know where her spot was. As if I didn't know where all her spots were.

While I feasted and groaned over how good she tasted, Molli panted and tried to push my head back.

"Grayson, yes," she moaned. Hearing her moan my name reset my stamina every time.

I tapped the side of her thigh with two fingers, and she knew to flip over onto her stomach. Molli's body was warm, with most of the heat coming from her inner thighs.

"I love you," I spoke in her ear, my bottom lip brushing against her diamond earring. "I appreciate you for taking care of me last night."

"My pleasure," she whispered, turning her head to request my lips on hers. And I chuckled, because it was definitely about to be all pleasure for her. "I love you too."

Molli turned on her back again, pulling me on top of her. Her strength overpowered mine this morning. My hangover wasn't playing fair and neither was she.

In her arms, she held me against her and grabbed my hard dick. One of her soft hands rubbed up and down my dick as the other massaged my balls.

"Lay back and relax." She kissed my cheek and reached into the nightstand on her side of the bed. Her right hand never left my balls; she held me hostage by them. "Your eyes. Close them."

"What are you trying to do to me, woman?" I asked, closing my eyes at the same time. Whatever she wanted from me, she effortlessly got. "Shit," I groaned when her hand returned to my dick. She covered the head of it with lube, smothering the cool, tingling sensation over it. "Mol—"

"Keep your eyes closed," she whispered. "I told you to relax."

At this point, I didn't have a choice. Her hand moving up and down my dick crippled me. She didn't let up as both hands put in work to weaken me. Applying pressure to my balls, she squeezed them and moaned in my ear.

"Sometimes I just want to please you," she said, her tongue teasing the inside of my ear.

"Shit," I grumbled under my breath. I was trying to hold on, but she knew what was up. Molli knew what the fuck she was doing. She was the type who was good at any and everything she put her mind to.

A wave of jealousy over the niggas she'd been with in the past washed over me. I'd lucked up in all areas with her, and no one would ever have her again.

Her heart belonged to me, and I was grateful whenever she told me her soul, body and pussy was mine, too.

"I want to see you do it. Come for me."

Her sexy voice in my ear got her exactly what she

wanted. I groaned as my dick erupted all over her hand. She stroked through the eruption until my body jerked forward and she knew I couldn't take anymore.

"Fuck!" My chest heaved as I tried to catch my breath.

"Stay put." She kissed my cheek and slid out of bed. "I'll be back to clean you up. I'm going to take care of you today." She licked her fingers and smiled just before disappearing into the bathroom.

I knew all along that Molli was a dangerous woman. Dangerous in the best, unpredictable, and most remarkable ways.

Damn.

"THANK YOU FOR COMING," GIANNA SAID AS I SLID across from her and Xavier in the booth. I nodded to acknowledge him, then looked at Gianna like she was crazy.

Thank you for coming.

That shit irritated me. She knew I would always run when she called. Whether we were on shaky terms or not, I would always show up for her.

"Welcome to Highland Coffee Shop, sir," a chipper, blonde barista approached the booth. She set a strawberry banana smoothie and spinach and feta sandwich in front of Gianna—her favorite combination to have at Highland Coffee Shop since she was thirteen. Any time I used to visit the crib to check on her and our parents, she begged me to take her there for a fix.

"Your strawberry banana smoothie and spinach, feta panini," the barista confirmed Gianna's order and smiled. "Can I get you guys anything?" She looked back and forth from me and Xavier.

"I'm good, thanks." I nodded, returning a forced smile.

"Same here. Thank you," Xavier said.

"No problem at all. Wave me down if you need anything else." She walked away, and I shifted in my seat.

I waited impatiently for Gianna to tell me what she wanted to talk to me about. Last time I'd saw and talked to her, she stormed out of my condo after dropping an abortion bomb on me. I woke up this morning assuming she and Xavier were halfway back to Miami already. To my surprise, she responded to my safe travels text with a location to meet up, saying she really needed to talk to me before she left.

As always, I came running.

"Y'all good?" I asked, looking from her to Xavier.

Xavier nodded. "Yeah, man. You?"

"As good as I'm gon' get," I said.

Gianna's curls were pinned up, displaying her full, round face. She looked so much like our mother that it was hard being upset with her. Her beauty was fresh, and her essence was pure. I was thirteen when my parents brought her home and laid her in my arms to video record and take pictures of us together. I stared into her face and called her my angel that day.

Why'd she have to grow up on me like that?

"Grayson, I'm sorry for how I spoke to you and stormed out the other night." While she spoke, all I saw was the top of her head. Gianna stared down at her smoothie, fiddling with the straw she'd dipped in the top of the large, plastic cup. "Disrespecting you is the last thing I ever want to do. I look up to you and I only ever want to make you proud. I thought..." she paused and wiped her eyes with the back of her hands. "I thought you would be somewhat okay with the idea. I thought you would've wanted us to focus on school and—"

"Gianna there's no way you thought I wanted

you to get rid of your baby. Is that what you're telling me?"

"Can you let her talk?" Xavier stepped in. I couldn't help the scowl that took over my face, or my eyes that cut at him. "It's no disrespect on my end, man. She just needs to get it out the best way she knows how."

"You got it." I sat back and said.

On one hand, I was inclined to ask him who the fuck he thought he was talking to. Perhaps even grab his ear and drag him out of the coffee shop by his dangling cross earring. However, on the other hand, I liked that he had her back. For the way he loved, cared for, and stepped up to the plate for her, I respected him.

"Xavier and I are disappointed in ourselves for not being more careful. I thought aborting the baby would make everything go back to normal and..." she paused again, and her tears fell freely this time. Xavier whispered something in her ear, then wiped her tears. "I'm sorry I let you down and I love you. I couldn't go back to Miami without seeing you and telling you that."

"Are you going to look at me?" I asked, my eyes pinned on her. As much as I wanted to baby her, I couldn't anymore.

Looking up at me, she reached across the table for my hand. I grabbed her hand and huffed.

"You been stressing me out since Mom and Dad brought you home from the hospital, you know that?"

"Yeah, yeah. I wouldn't stop crying in your ear." She laughed. "You still called me your angel, though. Don't leave that part of the story out."

"I only what wants best for you, Gia. I'm going to be here to support you through it all. I'm going to be here to watch you bounce back every time you fall. I am always going to be here."

"Pinky promise." She held her pinky out and wiggled it like old times.

"Pinky promise," I said, wrapping my pinky around hers. "I can come to Miami with you. I'll pay for our flights and have Xavier's car delivered or I'll follow y'all—"

"I'm sorry but…" she paused and looked over at Xavier who already had his eyes on her. "This is something we want to do on our own… together," she explained while staring into his eyes.

"I respect that," I said.

With pleading eyes, she looked ahead at me again. "Please don't tell Mom and Dad."

"It's not my story to tell."

"Thank you," she whispered and took a sip from her smoothie. The conversation was slowing down between us, and everyone's body language was turning awkward. Nonetheless, I was grateful she'd hit me up to talk. Grateful we were on better terms than we'd left off on the other night. "As for Molli." She laughed until it faded into a smile.

"What about her?"

"She's… the most amazing person I've met in a while. Her kindness gives me faith in humanity. I could go on and on, but I think you already know how special she is. And I'm not just saying this because of everything she's done for me or how she's been there for me over the last few weeks. She really is amazing, Grayson. Treat her right."

"I plan on it,"

There was no way in hell I was letting Molli go. Good women like her were rare and once in a life-time experience. Fuck around and hurt a good woman like Molli if you wanted to, a great deal of pain and regret would follow you around for the rest of your life. No wonder her ex was suffering without her.

"Take care of my sister, X." I shook my deep thoughts of Molli and held my fist out to dap him up.

"With my life," he looked me in my eyes and promised.

I PROMISED I WOULD MEET MOLLI AT STARDUST lounge after seeing Gianna and Xavier off tonight.

Molli, her best friend, Jana, and Mona, had all talked their men into hitting up the lounge with them, just to watch them dance and giggle in the middle of dance floor. They didn't even notice that we'd arrived, and I had to introduce Don to Jana's boyfriend, Quinton. She was too busy swaying her hips with her girls on the dance floor to give them a proper introduction.

"Is it me or are they all matching?" Quinton asked, then threw back a shot of Hen. My hangover from this morning was still lingering. The thought of liquor made me cringe, let alone the smell. A bottle of water was the only thing helping me keep it together.

"Color coordinating and shit, and we're over here looking like their cheerleaders," Don said.

"I know y'all aren't up here bitching for real." I looked at them and laughed.

"Says the man who's in here with two bunches

of flowers, waiting for his girl to stop dancing and come to the bar!" Don scoffed. "Show off."

"Look at you. Loud, drunk and wrong. These are for the bouncer."

"What bouncer? I know you ain't talking about the wide body nigga who be standing outside the door." Quinton's eyebrow shot up.

"That's the one. It's 'bout to get busy soon. He should be clocking in at any minute now."

"Man, what the fuck you got going on? You got something you need to tell me?" Donovan side-eyed me.

"Yeah, and it won't be nice if you keep playing with me."

Donovan nudged Quinton and said, "He's always been sensitive." They both cackled like Don was a comedian, but I couldn't focus on that. The nigga I'd been scoping the scene for walked into the lounge, and I was ready to deliver his package back to him.

Kennan entered the lounge and his eyes immediately landed on Molli. He stood by the door and watched her as I watched him. I didn't blame him for admiring her, I blamed him for fucking up long ago and now trying to make up for it. His chances with her were over, and although he knew she was involved with someone else, he still sent those fucking flowers to her crib. I didn't appreciate that.

It was a shame how possessive I felt over Molli. I tried to simmer that shit down, but I couldn't. Kennan better had counted his blessings when he had her. He better had cherished those memories, because he would never have shorty again. Unlike him, fucking up wasn't on my agenda.

"I'll be back." I grabbed the flowers and headed in his direction with them hidden behind my back. Something told me he would head her way to speak to her soon. I had to make myself clear before he tried. "Ayo!" I shouted for his attention. He squinted his eyes in confusion until I was standing directly in front of him.

"What's up? I know you?" He asked, a sly smirk on his goofy ass face.

I laughed in his face. If it made him feel better to pretend that he didn't know who I was, so be it, that was on him.

"Now you do," I said, bringing the flowers from my back and pushing them into his chest. "Thanks for the heads up on what she likes, but I'll take over with making sure she receives them know. You can have these backs."

Kennan let them fall to his feet, but I didn't give

a fuck. They belonged to him now. After everything Molli told me about him, he was lucky I didn't drop him to the ground right next to them. He was lucky I didn't bury him alive and plant those shits on top of his grave.

"You better watch yourself man," he threatened loud and clear. We were eye-level with each other, neither of us willing to back down. The thoughts in my head were encouraging me to knock his ass out. I almost gave in, then Molli's small, sweet voice emitted as she grabbed my hand.

"Dance with me." She tugged on my arm, pulling me toward the dance floor. "He isn't worth the trouble." I looked down into her glowing brown eyes and smiled. She was so fucking beautiful that it blew my mind sometimes.

"Right," I said, glaring back up at him. "Not worthy of you either." I took small steps back as she led us onto the dance floor. I never broke eye contact with him until he stormed out of the lounge pissed off.

The band slowed down their jazz rhythm, and Molli reached up and wrapped her arms around my neck.

"You are so bad." She shook her head. "Why'd you do that?"

"I needed to kill any ounce of hope he had." I shrugged. "Besides, he disrespected me. He knew what was up with us and tried to get at you anyway."

"Are you saying you would've fought for me, Mr. Steel?" She blushed, pulling me lower for a kiss.

"Without a second thought about it." I kissed her bottom lip before taking it into my mouth. "Believe that," I pulled away and mumbled against her lips.

"How's Gianna?"

"She's... better. We don't have to talk about that anymore. I'm sorry you were pulled into our—"

"Don't do that," she said, stopping us from swaying slowly on the dance floor. We stood in place, gazing into each other's eyes for answers or whatever came next.

"I know she's taken over our world this past week, but I feel..." Molli sighed and dropped her eyes to my chest.

"Look at me. Tell me what you feel," I requested.

"In a way, I feel like it was what we needed. It brought us closer together and we learned things about each other that only we know now. I'm not happy she's going through this, you know? I'm just thankful I got to be there for her, bring y'all together, and gain more of you in the process. And you, me. You definitely have more of me now. All of me."

"I feel that," I said, pushing her hair out of her face to get a clear look at her.

The lounge was dim yet blinding with florescent lights flashing above us. Still, her beauty was the most distracting thing in the room. All the conversations surrounding us were muted. Molli was the only person who mattered to me in this moment. The only force that captivated me entirely.

"You have no idea how grateful I am for you. I look back and don't know how I've remained sane without you."

Our lips met half-way, crashing into each other's. I pushed my tongue past her lips to taste her, wrapping my hand around her neck to deepen our kiss.

I never thought I could love this deeply. Now that I'd met Molli, considering a world without her was out of the question. I was holding on for dear life, and I would never let go.

The sound of our names over the mic broke our mutual trance. We forced ourselves to pull away from each other and face the stage.

"This is for Molli and Grayson. For Mona and Donovan. For me and Quinton," Jana spoke into the mic. She settled on a stool in front of the mic and looked back at the band, nodding for them to follow her lead.

"Go best friend. That's my best friend. That's my best friend!" Molli cheered her on until a soft melody commenced in the background. Jana hummed into the mic, then closed her eyes to sing:

No more lonely, no more just me

I've been there before, ain't goin' no more

And now that you're here, I never wanna say goodbye, love

Never wanna be without you

No more crying', no denyin'

I'm in love with you

And now that you're here, I never wanna say goodbye.

While every couple in attendance were cuddled together during her performance, Quinton stood in front of the stage, staring at her pour her heart out. A couple feet beside him, Mona and Donovan were lost in each other. Mona held both sides of Don's face as they smiled at each other and rocked from side to side, in tune with the band's rhythm.

I cupped Molli's face and leaned down to kiss her wet cheek. "Why are you crying?"

"I'm happy," she whispered.

"Just checking," I said, embracing her securely in my arms. "That's all I want to do." I squeezed her ass through her painted-on jeans. We would have to discuss them and the tight crop top that outlined every curve on her body later. She was too fine to be coming to the lounge like that. No wonder Kennan was losing his mind and trying to bag her back.

"Mark my words, I'll never stop making you happy."

"I second that."

Cheers erupted after Jana finished her performance. Molli used their distraction to her advantage. She dug her hand in my pants and grabbed my dick through my briefs. "Let's go home."

I chuckled. "Nasty ass."

Home—whether mine or hers—was wherever she was.

```
Epilogue
MOLLI
```

Release Day…

"It's only midnight, Molli. Oh my God! You're already in the top ten for new thriller releases," Mona screamed in my ear. "It hasn't even been out for five hours."

While on a three-way call with my sisters, I paced back and forth in my bedroom, trying to avoid grabbing my laptop and stalking posts online about my latest novel, *A World of Secrets*. That wasn't the only thing I tried to avoid; my night had become more complex than I expected.

"It's that amazing ass cover," I got out of my head and said. "They're drawn to it."

"Girlfriend, it's that amazing ass writing," Monika corrected.

"That amazing ass cover combined with that amazing ass writing," Mona corrected us both. "This is amazing. You did it again."

"We did it again," I said. "You help me with my finances and Monika helps me with my graphics. I'm lucky to have you two. We're a team."

"That, we are," Monika said. "I'm going to get some shut eye. I love you both. Congratulations again, Mol. You're a rock star."

"Love you too! Goodnight," Mona and I sang in unison.

When we were younger, every time we'd accomplish anything or did a good deed, our father deemed us *rock stars*. Even the simplest things brought us the title. Long as we were progressing, we were his rock star daughters.

I couldn't wait to purchase Dad another baseball collective's item to celebrate. That was how I personally celebrated with him. I'd deliver the item to him the same day it arrived at my house, and while he shined it and added it to his collection, we discussed everything about my latest release and what ideas I had up my sleeve for the next one.

Morris Hill was my favorite human. My mom respected that I was a daddy's girl. I made it up to her by helping her with her garden every time I visited. They'd preferred we visit more often, like every day if it were up to them. But as long as me and my sisters remained close to each other, our unity satisfied them more than anything else.

"Mol," Mona shouted my name, snapping me out of my rapid, random thoughts and stopping me in my tracks from pacing.

"Y-yes. I'm still here. Sorry I zoned out."

"Get out of your head and be proud of yourself. Enjoy this moment."

I exhaled deeply and nodded like she could see me. "Thank you, sis. I love you."

"Love you more. Want me to come over? We can drink Dom, stuff our faces with processed foods and dance."

I held back from telling her that I probably wouldn't be drinking Dom again anytime soon. Instead, I laughed and looked up from my freshly pedicured toes. The man who helped me choose the cotton-candy pink color via text message earlier had arrived.

Grayson leaned against the threshold with a subtle grin on his handsome face. His fitted Powell's Southern Smokehouse T-shirt exposed his broad, buff shoulders, and I couldn't wait to wrap my arms around them.

"How does tomorrow sound?" I asked Mona.

"Like your man just got there. Donovan's on the way so it's all good. Tomorrow?"

"Tomorrow," I confirmed. "Goodnight."

"Goodnight, best seller," she said and disconnected our call.

Placing my phone on the dresser, I walked into his arms, airing a sigh of relief against his chest. I never imagined it to be possible, but my happiness was overwhelming me. It overpowered my anxiety, but I still didn't know what to do with myself. Pinching myself was out of the question. Even if it was a dream, I wanted to live it out. I deserved it.

"Congratulations, beautiful," he lifted my chin with two fingers and said.

"How'd you... I haven't even told you the good news yet."

"Don't you know by now that I keep up with you, woman?" A gentle kiss to my collarbone sent chills down my spine. "How should we celebrate tonight? You can have whatever you want."

"Good, because I just want to be in your arms tonight," I said, caressing his silky, dark cocoa skin.

"Done." Grayson's large, warm hands travelled underneath my short, black, lace night gown. His eyes lit up when he discovered I had on a mini G-string.

Tongue-kissing my neck, he slapped my ass, then pulled back to control himself. "I'ma hit the shower. I'll be back."

"Hurry back." I lifted my gown to give him a better view.

"You'll regret teasing me later," he threatened and ducked off into the bathroom.

I stood in place until the shower started, then darted out of my bedroom.

In the bathroom of my guest room, two pregnancy tests that I'd been avoiding for the last hour awaited me. Though I was nervous and anxious over the results, I already knew what they were.

My period was three weeks late. Birth control had always thrown my menstrual cycle off a bit, but not like this. Forgetting to take the pill some days had caught up to me, and now, we no longer had a Gianna dilemma, we had our own circumstance to tend to.

"God!" I covered my mouth and gasped, tears instantly welling in my eyes. Both tests displayed two, dark red lines. My heart raced at the same time my world spun out of control. My sisters were going to have a field day with this one.

Grabbing a Ziplock bag from underneath the sink, I stored the positive tests inside of it, washed my hands, and then returned to my bedroom with them behind my back.

On the verge of hyperventilating, I took a deep breath and stood in front of the end of the bed, waiting on Grayson to come out of the bathroom.

Twenty long minutes felt like five hours had passed. He'd been on the other side of the bathroom door with no idea that I was going crazy.

"Mol!" Grayson barged out of the bathroom with a damp towel around his waist. Beads of water trickled down his enticing chest. Approaching me with his phone in his hand, he held it out for me to read a text on the screen. "She's keeping it," he said. "Gianna's keeping the baby. I'm going to be an uncle." Lifting me in his arms, he whisked me around the room, then sat me on the edge of the dresser. His excitement over the good news warned my heart. I prayed I didn't ruin it with the bomb I was about to drop on him.

"What's this?" He picked up the Ziplock bag I'd dropped and examined the tests through the clear bag.

"You're going to be an uncle and a father," I whispered.

His silence scared me, then a tear fell from his eye and he tried to drop his head.

Jumping down from the dresser, I cupped both sides of his face, swiping his tear away with my thumb.

"You're crying?" I asked, holding back tears of my own. "Why?"

"I'm happy," he said.

"We just confirmed our relationship and—"

"And what? You don't want this or something?" His body tensed up and he almost backed away from me, but I held onto him. I kept his face in my hands, swiping away tears that fell out of his control. My heart performed flips inside my chest. I didn't have to question if Grayson wanted this, I could already tell he did. More than anything else, he wanted this.

"I do. I just wondered if you were, you know, ready."

"Molli," he sighed and embraced me tightly in his arms. "I'm ready for everything with you," he confessed. "Haven't I been showing you that?"

"Yes," I whispered. "You have."

"Besides, it's like you said..." He backed me against the bed until I fell back on it. Pulling me to the edge of the bed, he spread my legs. "Everything happened the way it was supposed to." He kissed my inner thighs and I giggled from the tickling sensation of his wet beard.

"Do you think our love will last forever?" I asked, moaning as he dropped to his knees to roll his tongue over my pulsating clit. "Grayson," I moaned and whimpered. "I want forever with you."

"Everlasting," he spoke against my clit, groaning like I was the best thing he'd ever indulged in. "That's what our love is, woman. *Act like you know.* Isn't that what you always tell me?"

"Oh, yes." I panted as he found my spot with his tongue and pushed a finger inside of me. My pussy gushed for him, and he was having the time of his life between my thighs.

"Repeat it back to me," he demanded.

"Our love is everlasting," I moaned. "I love you so much, Grayson." I rubbed through his hair as a body trembling orgasm ripped through me. My body convulsed, and he held onto me by my waist, still groaning as he kissed my pussy lips.

"Everlasting," he repeated.

THE END

Also by ShanicexLola

Are you all caught up on **Mona x Donovan?** Read the first Hill Sisters book here: http://bit.ly/guardedbylove

Want more of **Jana x Quinton?** Read their novelette here: https://bit.ly/impassionedintentions

Author's Note

Thank you for reaching the end of Molli x Grayson's story. If you've enjoyed this book, please consider leaving a review on Amazon + Goodreads

Here are some goodies to enjoy: **Everlasting Love's Apple Music Playlist:** https://music.apple.com/us/playlist/everlasting-love/pl.u-4JommaGtdj0Z4d

Everlasting Love's Pinterest Board: https://pin.it/5lJtnpi

Join us in my readers group on Facebook to share your thoughts on Everlasting Love: http://bit.ly/ShaniceRomanticHaven

You can also connect with me on my personal Facebook here: http://bit.ly/FBShaniceSwint

To be the first to know of new releases, cover

reveals, giveaways and more, subscribe to my mailing list here: http://eepurl.com/dsb1EL

Again, thank you so much for indulging in Molli x Grayson story! I can't wait to hear from you.

xoxo, ShanicexLola

CPSIA information can be obtained
at www.ICGtesting.com
Printed in the USA
LVHW051946171220
674450LV00014B/1515